# LAST SHIELD

### EMMA LAST SERIES: BOOK FOURTEEN

MARY STONE

Copyright © 2025 by Mary Stone Publishing

All rights reserved.

No part of this book may be reproduced in any form or by any electronic or mechanical means, including information storage and retrieval systems, without written permission from the author, except for the use of brief quotations in a book review.

❦ Created with Vellum

*To the officers who serve with honor, who stand for justice when it's hard, and who protect without praise—thank you. This story may blur the lines, but you are the reason we sleep soundly.*

# DESCRIPTION

**The past has a pulse. And it's hunting her.**

FBI Special Agent Emma Last is still trying to catch her breath after what went down in Salem. The trauma lingers. The secrets she's held tight? Not so secret anymore. And as her team reels from the fallout, her once-solid foundation is starting to crack.

And that's not even the worst of it.

When a rookie DC cop is gunned down in a federal garage by someone wearing an FBI windbreaker, the storm only intensifies. The killer might be posing as one of their own—or worse, might actually be one of them. Before Emma can make sense of the ambush, another officer's gunned down.

Now it's not just murder—it's a message.

The media is circling. Tensions are high. And the arrival of a new agent with a murky past is the last thing she needs.

As questions mount and alliances shift, Emma must navigate a minefield of suspicion, betrayal, and a personal vendetta that may trace back to a sister she's never met. One with a dangerous grudge—and a growing body count.

**Last Shield, the gripping fourteenth book in the Emma Last FBI series by bestselling author Mary Stone, is a razor-sharp psychological thriller where trust can be weaponized—and the enemy might already be inside the circle.**

# 1

Officer Greg Darby turned onto Architect Street, nearing the edge of his patrol sector. Seedy businesses and empty lots surrounded him, but he wasn't worried. This area was dead after midnight and not much trouble before. Ahead of him, testament to the thought, the street sat clear and empty other than a garbage truck. The sight was familiar. Par for the course at five on a Monday morning.

*Once some new rookies come in, maybe I'll have a chance at a better beat.*

After nights, weeks, and months spent processing drunk-and-disorderlies, public urination, and disturbing the peace, it wasn't the first time that sentiment had crossed Greg's mind.

But how long could the chief expect him to sit on the night shift? He'd been a cop for a year already, but he felt more like a bouncer most of the time.

Greg turned at the end of the block, sipping from the dregs of his coffee. The night would be over soon, at least. With the bars closed, he was well into the boring part of his shift. It would soon change over to early-morning-commute fender benders.

Meanwhile, he'd make a stop at the all-night gas station on Kingston Street and get a fresh cup of coffee. The station was across from an all-night local bail bond business. The place sported some interesting characters, so who knew?

*Any luck, I might find someone breaking the law and make an actual fucking arrest.*

The sarcasm didn't ring true in his heart. He wasn't that far gone yet. But he was well past understanding why so many cops on the force became jaded with police work long before they got the chance to earn a sergeant badge. For that reason, he had a side hustle in the works, doing real police work that fed his overarching purpose for getting into the law—to make the world a better place. But who knew when he'd get his big break in that case?

Rather than further indulge in pessimism, he picked up his radio. "Dispatch, Patrol 85. Taking Code 7 at Brew-and-Go on Kingston. Back in three."

After a few seconds, Cindy's tired voice came through. "Copy, Patrol 85."

Just ahead, a figure stepped out into the road, waving his arms. Slowing, Greg squinted through the dirty windshield, taking the man in. The lights from the Brew-and-Go created a neon halo, highlighting an FBI windbreaker and dark slacks. A dark ball cap sporting Bureau letters indicated this was the real deal.

*Young, clean-cut, fit, and professional enough to be a Fed but also agitated and out of place.*

On high alert, Greg pulled to the side of the road beneath a streetlight by a condemned car wash and rolled his window down just as the Fed jogged over. The man flashed his badge before he got to the car.

"Officer, I'm glad you showed up. I could use some help."

Putting the cruiser in park, Greg eyed the badge closely. He had big dreams of joining the elite unit one day and had studied enough pictures to know this one was authentic. The morning was turning out to be eventful, after all. "Officer Darby out of the Eighth, how can I help, Agent…?"

"Special Agent Ron Knight." The man stuck his hand through the open window, awkward as all get-out, but Greg twisted in his seat to shake it anyway. "Look, I gotta get to Richmond with some evidence before the courthouse opens, and my partner cleared out to tackle another call. I've got some boxes that're gonna take two people to carry. Could you do me a solid and help out? I'll put in a call to Chief Ebenstein and tell him you saved my hide."

Greg gazed longingly at the Brew-and-Go before nodding. The last thing he wanted to do was cause a scene or, worse, get flagged as an asshole if this guy called up Chief Ebenstein. The guy's windbreaker practically glowed under the streetlight, his Fed cover advertising his identity to anyone who glanced over.

"Yeah, man, I've got some time. Let me park."

The agent stepped back up onto the sidewalk, spewing thanks, and Greg pulled up against the curb.

Leaving his patrol car to lug around boxes like a Fed's lackey wasn't exactly the change of pace he'd been looking for, but it couldn't hurt to help the guy out. Then he'd get his coffee, and soon enough, there'd be another night on the books.

He glanced at his car radio. Technically, he was on break, and technically, he should report a change in location.

Greg reached for the mic just as dispatch lit up, fast and frantic—overlapping voices, clipped codes, and background sirens. Sounded like a pileup near the expressway.

He waited through several moments of back-and-forth, thumb resting on the button, watching the Fed out of the corner of his eye. The guy glanced at his watch, looked around, and ran a hand through his hair. He was clearly in a hurry.

*Dammit.*

Dispatch stayed jammed.

Greg let out a quiet breath. This wouldn't take more than a few minutes, and he was less than half a block from where he'd reported to be going. He'd likely be back in range by the time the lines cleared. Besides, his radio was on his belt if anyone needed him.

Agent Knight adjusted his jacket, grinning like he'd just won the lottery, and Greg followed him past the run-down bail bond office. The owner was moving around inside. Greg gave the guy's back a sarcastic wave as they passed.

When they came to the alley on the other side of the business, Greg slowed. The alley was short, but still—something about leaving the streetlights behind scraped at his nerves. He wasn't about to walk into a dead zone without asking questions.

"Agent Knight, you know I'm on duty, right? How far are we going?"

Knight waved a hand like it was no big deal. "Just down the alley. See that garage?"

Greg didn't move. He scanned the shadows, took in the federal parking garage, and cracked his neck. *Fine.* But in case this went south, he was already counting exits.

The garage was attached to the recently closed Capitol Bank, and Greg glanced around as they moved up to the entrance. "How'd you end up with evidence here?"

"It's old bank files from a fraud case. White-collar crime. Not why I got into the FBI, but it's a start. I got the key to the office and was told to pick 'em up this morning." The agent grimaced as he held the side door entrance, intended for pedestrians, open for Greg.

Greg studied him. "You hurt?"

Knight patted his ribs. "Cracked a couple ribs during an asset seizure…fraud case out in Riverview. The guy had a panic room, two pit bulls, and a serious attitude about his frozen accounts."

Greg laughed. "Always the white-collar ones that lose it hardest."

"Right? Give me a guy with a gun over a hedge fund manager with nothing to lose any day." Knight smiled like he didn't love the attention but couldn't help the pride that crept in. "Didn't think the guy would launch off a loading dock, but hey, we got him."

Greg nodded, a bit of that professional suspicion melting away. He remembered that takedown. Heard it on the local news.

"All right," he rubbed his hands together, stepping past the agent and into the garage. "Let's move some files."

Knight chuckled. "Nobody told me that one box would weigh a ton and the other would be six feet long, or I'd have brought help. When I spotted your cruiser, I couldn't believe my luck."

Greg shrugged off the repeated thanks as he moved toward the glassed-in entrance to the bank just across the lot. The echo of his boots rang hollow. When no footsteps joined in, he stopped cold. His hand went to his sidearm before he even turned. The sudden stillness raised every hair on his arms.

He twisted around. The agent's silhouette stood clear in the dim light, arm extended, gun drawn.

*Shit. Should've called it in. Should've followed the damn protocol. Shouldn't have been so fucking stupid.*

Instinct kicked in. Greg pivoted hard, foot scraping concrete, body launching sideways. No cover except that waist-high divider. Not enough, but better than open ground. If he made it there, he'd have a shot—literally.

Gunfire cracked behind him.

He hit the ground in a roll, shoulder screaming, the wind knocked clean out of him. Came up in a crouch, weapon drawn, scanning the area. Thankful for his vest.

"Knight...whatever the hell your name is, drop it!"

No answer. Just the whisper of movement and then—

*Crack.*

Pain bloomed along the side of Greg's head and ear. His hearing went sideways, muffled and ringing. Warmth poured down his neck, slipping through his fingers as he attempted to staunch the flow. He staggered, bracing against the divider, weapon trembling in his grip.

*Ear's gone. Or mostly. Doesn't matter.*

He gritted his teeth, forced his focus forward, trying to track the shooter through the haze. The Fed—no, the *fake*—was already retreating, silhouette vanishing through the shadows like a ghost.

*Because I'm already dead.*

To hell with that.

Greg tried to raise his gun again, but his arm wouldn't listen. The world was slipping sideways, angles turning wrong. He fumbled for the radio. Missed. Tried again.

Didn't matter. Not enough time.

Thoughts fired off in fragments—images more than words.

The girl at the coffee shop. Alina. That shy little smile she gave him when he made her laugh last time he was there.

His mom, baking cinnamon rolls on Sundays, even after he moved out.

His brother with the stupid tattoos.

The dog he swore he'd adopt when he finally had a backyard.

He wasn't done. Not even close.

Greg clenched his jaw, trying to hold on to something—anything—but his knees buckled, body folding against the divider. His gun hit the concrete, skittered out of reach.

Above him, the darkened rafters blurred and bent as his vision tunneled. Somewhere in the distance, a siren wailed. Too far. Too late.

Greg Darby, fighter to the end, let out one last breath and slumped to the floor—*not* because he gave up, but because he ran out of time.

## 2

Special Agent Emma Last reeled at what her SSA had told her just a half hour ago.

Even now, staring at the picture of her younger self, a fresh graduate from Quantico, she couldn't understand why a maniac had possessed *that* particular photo.

She remembered the moment it was taken—studio lights in her eyes, a brand-new suit, her father's proud smile behind the cameraperson. It was a memory she used to hold close.

Now it was evidence.

Her supervisory special agent's words still echoed, low and steady. *"I hate to say it...you're a target."*

Emma blinked and refocused on Renee Bailey's monitor. One half of the screen held the image of the photo—her face, her past. The other showed the handwriting on the back.

*Emma Marie Last*, written in someone else's hand.

Neat. Precise. Not her father's.

"Loop in the *R* is a little high." The resident linguist zoomed in on the exact spot she was referring to. "Feminine, probably. And whoever wrote this? Not in a rush. Confident stroke."

Emma didn't respond. Her thoughts were still tangled in the conversation that had led her here. How the team had confirmed the emails in the last case weren't written by the perpetrator of such violent acts as killing gang members and slicing off their tattoos. How the language had shifted…

*…tide of vermin…useless leeches…*

How someone else, someone hidden, had likely pulled the strings from the shadows.

Someone who had paid Special Agent Vance Jessup's kidnapper a small fortune. Someone who had access to Emma's life—*and her past.*

She wrapped her hands around her coffee mug, more for grounding than warmth.

Whoever this woman was, she hadn't just targeted victims. She'd targeted *Emma.*

*"You're a target."*

Not maybe. Not possibly. *You are.*

And then there was him. The killer she'd brought down.

She couldn't forget the way the air had shifted around her —how the temperature dropped like the universe had stopped breathing.

One minute, she was yelling at him to stay on the ground and drop his weapon. The next, the dead man was standing in front of her.

*"A storm sent me for you, Special Agent Emma Marie Last. And it's still coming. This is your last sign."*

The words haunted her almost as much as the way he'd known her full name.

Her *full* name.

Not even Celeste had used that.

Emma shook off the chill crawling up her spine.

The emails. The money. The sister. The damn graduation photo. And then a ghost with a half-blown-off skull telling her the clock was ticking.

It was all driving her crazy.

Emma shut out the noise in her mind. Theories and fear could come later. Right now, she needed facts.

"As I mentioned the last time we met, this looks like the handwriting from our perpetrator's journals." Renee's expression was filled with compassion.

Emma sighed, knowing that Renee wouldn't have changed her analysis, no matter how much she might hope for it.

A pair of anonymous, threatening emails were central to their last case. At first, the emails had appeared to be from one perpetrator—a man determined to rid the D.C. area of gang "cockroaches." But upon further study, it seemed another author, with a much more sinister motive toward Emma, was in play.

"We still don't have an identity on who sent these." Renee pulled up the emails, which didn't seem to match their Bug Man perpetrator. "I checked with Cyber before coming here, and they didn't have an IP yet or anything else that might be helpful. So right now, we're running solely on linguistic comparisons to prove a different email author."

Nodding along, Emma searched the texts for more details on the potential email author—the mystery woman who might have set the Bug Man loose. "Have you discovered anything new about the sender?"

"The sentence construction is clean and fairly complex, suggesting a high level of education. They sound professional, and while there aren't *many* regional indicators, the syntax and vocab choices are consistent with a resident of New England." Renee frowned at the screen. "But, of course, that could mean someone was raised and educated on the East Coast but moved away later, so you can't put too much focus on that when it comes to nailing location."

A little flutter of disappointment sent Emma sitting back in her seat, resting against the soft afghan that brought an extra flash of color to the office. "And that's it? That's all we can get?"

Renee pursed her lips in sympathy. "I'm sorry. All I can tell you is that I'm still doing research. I'll let you know if anything else comes up, though. I know how important this is."

"Thanks." Emma offered a smile to soften the disappointment she hadn't managed to contain. Renee re-angled her monitor to face her, and Emma headed out into the hall with a quick wave.

The photograph and strange woman serving as puppet master to their previous perpetrator bothered Emma more than she wanted to admit. There was only one person she could think of who might wish her ill—a possible sister.

A few weeks ago, back in Salem, Emma had been forced to kill a cop. She took a deep breath, letting the reminder settle in. She still couldn't believe it had all been real.

Making matters even worse, it wasn't just any cop. It was Celeste Foss, a childhood friend of her mother's. A woman twisted by years of jealousy, corruption, and something darker. The confrontation had been brutal. Personal. By the end, only one of them walked away.

But before Celeste died, she whispered something that still stuck like glass under Emma's skin.

*"When your sister learns of what you've done to me... she will find you, and she will end you."*

The words echoed even now, two states and a dozen nightmares later.

Emma wasn't sure what bothered her more—that she might have a sister she never knew about…or that she couldn't shake the idea the woman was already hunting her.

She hadn't found proof. No birth records. No DNA match. Nothing concrete to say, *yes, she exists.*

But Celeste wouldn't have said it for nothing.

Would she?

Maybe it was paranoia. Maybe the trauma had Emma seeing shadows in her own mind.

Or maybe Celeste knew *exactly* what she was doing—planting the seed and walking away with a final win, even in death.

If that was the evil woman's intentions, mission accomplished.

*If I do have a sister, she'd certainly have enough of a connection to me for a vendetta to have formed, whatever reasoning Celeste brainwashed her with.*

Emma jabbed the elevator button harder than she needed to. Metal groaned as the doors creaked open. She stepped inside and leaned against the wall, the box humming around her like it was holding its breath.

*If there is a sister...and she believes whatever lies Celeste fed her...*

Emma exhaled slowly through her nose.

*I'll find her before she finds me.*

The truth was, she'd already searched for all the information she could about her parents, as well as her mother's closest childhood friends, the ones from the picture who'd so recently messed with her life. She'd found no signs of hidden property or family, let alone anything like birth records for a long-lost sibling.

Even the records on Celeste Foss and Monique Varley, another of her mother's childhood friends, had turned up nothing but crickets. Both women had mostly stayed offline and kept to themselves. Neither had any remaining family—not that Emma could find—and her own parents had led clean and simple lives if she went by government records rather than witches' words.

Still, Emma had to do something.

Once back at her own desk in the bullpen of the Violent Crimes Unit, she pulled up the employment and tax records of everyone she'd been researching, cross-checking them with addresses, aliases, and anything that might crack the door open.

If she *did* have a sister, it made sense—on paper at least—that her father would've been the parent. Her mother had died while Emma was so young. No time for her to have had another secret child.

But the logic didn't sit clean. Emma had never found a single thread tying her dad to the Other, to Monique Varley, or to Celeste Foss. No connections. No whispers. No reason to think he'd been involved in any of it.

Still…what other explanation was there?

Unless someone had been hiding a sibling from the start. Or unless her mother's past before Emma's birth was a hell of a lot darker than she realized.

Emma began poring over her dad's employment records anew.

The PDFs with Celeste's background kept glaring at her from their minimized locations on her screen, though.

Giving up on Charles Last's history, Emma pulled up Celeste Foss's and reread the paperwork. Something in there had to tell her something, because she still couldn't help thinking this was all connected.

The latest reports were all related to the recently uncovered scandal of Detective Celeste Foss slowly draining the Salem armory for years. The woman had taken so many weapons that the Salem PD might never find them all again. Especially after Celeste set fire to the department to cover her tracks.

Celeste had been capable of playing pretend. And she'd been a good friend—as far as Emma knew—to Monique and to Emma's mother for years before going bad. The potential for evil must've been lurking in her. And she *was* evil. Would she have used that trickery to turn a sibling against Emma somehow? Assuming she existed, of course.

*But why the secrecy? Dad would've told me. Right?*

And what were the chances that Emma's only family would somehow be connected to the nefarious hand that wrote those emails in their current case?

"I'm grasping at straws here." Emma couldn't shake the feeling that the events that took place in Salem had somehow followed her back home.

And Jacinda believed it too. She didn't want any of them working alone, especially Emma, which meant she also felt an unexplained connection.

Maybe she'd call Marigold after work. Perhaps her psychic friend would have a way of ascertaining this *sister* situation.

Footsteps dragged Emma's attention toward the door. Special Agent Mia Logan had a coffee in one hand and her phone in the other, and she was walking fast. She glanced past Emma to the conference room. "Are we the first ones to get back here?"

SSA Hollingsworth chose that moment to push the door to her office open, waving at Emma. "I didn't text you because I knew you were already around. But new meeting. Now."

The elevator dinged, and Special Agents Leo Ambrose and Vance Jessup appeared in the hall a second later, both wearing frowns.

Dread filled Emma as she stood. This couldn't be good. "What'd I miss?"

Mia leaned in, talking as Jacinda beelined for the

conference room. "A rookie cop was murdered earlier this morning in a federal parking garage. A witness saw an FBI agent with him right before that."

Emma stared for a second, then bit back a groan and grabbed her tablet.

*So much for a slow day of research.*

# 3

Emma settled back into her seat at the conference table she'd just vacated barely an hour ago and opened her tablet, her attention only half on the screen.

Vance and Leo entered together, both dropping into chairs across from her and Mia. Leo offered a tired smile.

Vance's nod was tighter, distracted—but his gaze flicked toward Emma. "Long time no see."

It might've passed for a joke. Almost.

But his voice was rougher than usual, and the bruising across his jaw appeared even darker than they did a couple hours ago. The butterfly bandage on his temple caught the light every time he moved.

He didn't scowl. Didn't glare.

But he also didn't *really* look at her.

Not like he used to.

The Vance from before would've leaned back in his chair with a smart comment about the coffee. Maybe nudged her knee under the table, just to get her attention. This version just sat still, locked behind his injuries—and something else she couldn't quite name.

He'd apologized. Said they were cool. But something had shifted between then and now.

She tried to catch his eye, even mouthed, *You okay?* He didn't look her way again.

Oh, well. She'd ask him later.

Or not.

She honestly didn't know what she should do.

Across the table, Jacinda raked her fingers through her long red hair and let out a sharp breath.

Emma's gut tightened. If their SSA was already this annoyed, that didn't bode well.

"A rookie beat cop named Greg Darby was murdered early this morning." Jacinda touched a button on her laptop, and the ID of a smiling rookie in uniform appeared on the screen on the wall.

Emma couldn't help flinching. The muscular man in uniform looked straight off a recruiting poster, fresh-faced and so excited to wear the badge.

"Dispatch couldn't get ahold of him after he radioed in to report taking a coffee break. His car also hadn't moved since that check-in, so they sent another officer to investigate and found his unit near the federal parking garage attached to that Capitol Bank that closed last month."

"Like he was run off the road?" Vance rubbed the area around his bandage.

Jacinda shook her head. "No, like he decided to park just past the Brew-and-Go coffee shop against the curb and wander off. The fact that he didn't actually pull into the coffee shop's parking lot may or may not mean anything."

What could stop a beat cop at the end of an overnight shift from refueling on caffeine?

"A witness who works at the bail bond business near there said that he saw Darby get out of his car and walk down the alley to the garage, accompanied by a man in an

FBI windbreaker and cap. Darby's body was found in the parking garage when the investigating officers made a search of the area, but nobody's seen or been able to determine the identity of the FBI agent in question."

Leo leaned over the table. "Are we moving forward on the assumption that our unsub abducted the agent?"

Vance flinched, the reaction subtle but unmistakable. Across from him, Mia drew in a deep, quiet breath, steadying herself.

Emma's heart tugged for them both. A week ago, Vance had been the one taken—beaten and bloodied until they found him just in time. Mia, his partner in more ways than one, had unraveled during those endless hours, every second a countdown she couldn't stop. She, too, had suffered kidnapping on a different case not long ago.

The trauma had settled in all of them. Some days it just sat there. Other days—like this—it pressed on the bruise.

Jacinda shot each of them an apologetic look. "Right now, we're not carrying any assumptions. But no matter what, the fact that this crime took place on federal property means it is our case, regardless of whether we're looking at a real agent, fake agent, or kidnapped agent."

"Or all of the above?" Nobody smiled at Leo's half-hearted quip to lighten the mood.

Emma began taking notes, not wanting to dwell on the fact that two members of their team were abducted in the recent past. And now another agent might be in the same position.

Jacinda glanced at the picture of the deceased cop still gracing their screen. "We've got agents working to find out if any FBI agents are missing or unaccounted for, but so far, they're not coming up with anything. My phone will ring if they do. And if it doesn't? That means our agent could be an out-of-towner. And we won't know if he's gone missing, has been abducted, or is our unsub anytime soon."

Emma raised an eyebrow at the last option.

"This is the very *last* thing our team or the Bureau needs." Jacinda scanned the room. "I've gone to hell and back and sat my ass on Capitol Hill for two full days, trying to clear the air between law enforcement organizations and our government oversight, so an FBI agent implicated in an interagency murder is a massive step backward. Do I think a federal agent murdered this officer? No, I don't, and I doubt police or anyone else believes it, but it still doesn't look good."

"That's the understatement of the year." Mia grimaced, still focused on Officer Darby.

Jacinda's lips flattened. "Which is exactly why we need to take care of this quickly. Figure out what happened, catch our killer, write up the reports, and be done before local *or* national journalists start running articles."

Leo stole a gulp from his coffee. "I can only imagine what the media will say if they get their hands on this."

Emma waved to pull Jacinda's attention. "What about—"

"I don't know." Jacinda rubbed her temple. "Whatever you're about to ask, assuming it's about this case, the answer is that *I do not know*. That's all I've got, and what happens now is that we figure out the rest."

Closing her tablet cover, Emma nodded in acknowledgment.

"All right." Jacinda pushed back from the table, making it clear they were about to be dismissed. "Vance and Leo, you two go speak to Darby's coworkers and chief. Learn anything you can about his relationship to the FBI, whatever there might've been, and find out if anyone else might have a motive. Mia and Emma, the two of you head to the crime scene. I'd help if I could, but I'm dealing with internal issues right now."

Emma paused after standing. "Are we talking about internal issues related to Salem? Or the current case?"

"Yes." Jacinda pushed one hand through her hair again, and the move betrayed the fact that the SSA had used makeup to cover deep circles under her eyes.

Emma darted a look at Vance, whose grimace couldn't have been deeper.

**4**

Emma and Mia parked beside a forensic box truck, got out, and sidestepped a tech dusting the passenger side door of a black-and-white. He was taking fingerprints and didn't even bother looking up.

"More than due diligence." Emma gave the car a once-over. "Let's hope our unsub touched the cruiser when Darby pulled over."

Mia nodded as they moved away, up toward the officer guarding the alley. He didn't say a word while examining their identification. When he lifted the tape for her and Mia to step under, he remained flat-faced and grim.

*Bet he knew our victim. Someone to talk to later, maybe.*

She opened her mouth to offer condolences, but his radio sounded out for his attention.

*Later.*

Giving a brief glance back to the parked cruiser that now had the attention of two cops and a tech, Emma moved down the alley toward the garage. She wasn't surprised Jacinda had wanted them to park on this street instead of the next. Other than a few condemned buildings, a gas station, a coffee shop, and the bail bond place, not much occupied the block.

Mia leaned close to her shoulder. "If Darby parked by the coffee shop, he had to have a reason. You see anything that would make you stop there versus right here?"

Before entering the garage, Emma glanced back in the direction they'd come. She shook her head. "He wanted coffee, according to Dispatch, but there's no clear reason he wouldn't have then used the parking lot. And as a cop, he could've driven into this garage if he'd wanted to, right?"

Frowning, Mia nodded to a passing tech before focusing back on the vehicle entrance to the garage before them. "No reason not to drive right in that I can see."

Emma turned sideways and moved through the garage door, careful not to brush against the metal and potentially mar any fingerprints. Residue around the handle and door's edges proved techs had already dusted, but better safe than sorry.

Yellow evidence markers were scattered around the space. Emma watched her step. On foot, this was where the officer and FBI agent would've likely entered.

A plainclothes detective gestured them over to join him.

She and Mia moved forward to meet him beside the edge of a partition. Just beyond him, a tech stood over their victim. The tech was taking photos while another tech sketched the body in situ. The officer lay against the concrete barrier, as if someone had pushed him up against the half wall.

"I'm Special Agent Emma Last, and this is Special Agent Mia Logan." She gestured toward the fallen officer. "Did you know him personally?"

He held out his hand, shaking each of theirs before taking their cards. "Detective Mikey Horowitz, at your service. And, no, I didn't know him."

That was good. "What can you tell us?"

"From what we can tell, the officer got out of the car and headed down that alley with the agent our witness saw. Came in through the same side door you just entered. Before you ask, the tech dusted it for prints but didn't find any. There are no cars in the garage and weren't any here when the murder occurred."

This was also good news. "You accessed security footage?"

"Yeah, just a couple minutes ago. It's not much, but we ascertained that no vehicles drove in, and the only identifiable face is our victim's."

Reality poked a needle in the hope building inside Emma. Why couldn't a case be easy just once?

"The garage is federal property, right?"

Horowitz nodded at Emma's question. "But it's set to be decommissioned and sold to the city now that the IRS offices were relocated." He offered them an ironic smile. "Looks like it didn't get off the books fast enough. All your jurisdiction. This part of town is on the downswing. There should be better surveillance, but…there didn't seem to be much point."

A tech glanced up from a table set up for evidence, hazarding a wave before he went back to what he'd been doing.

Mia gazed over at the body, frowning. "Can we see the footage?"

"Oh, yeah, sure." Horowitz retrieved a tablet from the evidence table and led them over to a window ledge, where he set the tablet down and pulled up the footage.

It was gray and grainy but clear enough. Two men entered from the nearby entrance. Emma glanced back at it and immediately saw the little camera hanging above, aimed into the garage.

On the screen, the two men had barely made it inside—

with the cop walking ahead—when the agent raised a gun, pointing it at their officer's back.

Emma paused the footage, her breath momentarily stopped up in her lungs. "Wait. The agent shot him?"

Beside her, Mia's mouth hung open.

"Like I said, we just got access to the footage a couple minutes ago." Horowitz's nose wrinkled in obvious discomfort.

Emma waved him off, staying focused on the screen. The man in the FBI jacket and cap still held the gun on their cop's unsuspecting back. She pushed Play, and in another second, Darby twisted back around to face him. Their killer had either said something to draw his attention or done something to make him turn. Or maybe it was just the fact that he'd stopped walking.

The cop's eyes went wider than seemed possible when he realized what was happening. The gun jumped, and the officer stumbled sideways, moving fast. A second later, he was out of view. And then, like a panther, the agent followed Darby off camera.

A small halo effect showed up at the edge of the footage as a result of the agent firing his gun a second time.

Emma paused the video, glancing at the wall opposite the entrance. "I don't guess we have any sound?"

The detective shook his head.

"Our unsub would have to be standing almost over him to hit him because of that partition. Bullets don't go through concrete, last I heard." Mia walked closer to the half wall, examining the height and width.

Emma waited until she returned to their little group before pushing Play again. The alleged agent reappeared a few seconds later, head down and hustling, the FBI cap hiding his face entirely. And within seconds, he'd left by way of the door through which they'd entered.

Emma handed her card to the tech. "I need you to send me this footage."

*And then I'll send it to the rest of the team, but you can bet I'll warn them first.*

Her phone buzzed. Fast work. She typed a quick FYI about their shooter, attached the video, and uploaded it to the case file.

Horowitz jutted his chin over toward the victim. "If you don't have any more questions, and you want to see him, have at it. We're lucky. If Dispatch hadn't noticed his vehicle wasn't moving and sent someone out, the IRS folks would've stumbled upon him, and none of us would even be here yet."

*Lucky* wasn't the word Emma would use, but they were fortunate MPD monitored all beat officers with vehicular tracking, meaning Dispatch knew exactly where and when he'd stopped. It at least gave them a starting point to begin their search.

She led the way around the concrete partition and over to the victim, but she couldn't rid herself of the image of what had definitely looked like an FBI agent firing on a rookie cop.

The tech moved to meet them.

Officer Greg Darby stared up at nothing. His eyes and mouth were open in shock, and the fact that Emma could still remember the grin from his picture that morning made her heart ache.

His left ear was gone, along with part of his skull. Brain matter slicked the concrete, scattered like something wild had clawed through it. If he'd been conscious after the shot, it hadn't been for long. A few breaths, maybe. Just long enough to feel himself die.

Beside Darby's left leg, like a fistful of bread dunked in red sauce, there was the blob, a white ear jutting out through red and pink brain mush.

She bent to do him the justice of looking directly into his face before standing and turning to Mia. "So we know whoever killed him wanted him found soon, or at least wasn't all that *concerned* about when he'd be found."

Mia's gaze still rested on the victim. "And our unsub is either an agent or went to pains to make himself look like one."

A chill ran up Emma's back and across her neck, the air thickening and cooling around her. She turned in time to spot Officer Greg Darby's ghost appear from around the corner, coming up the ramp from the floor below. He appeared lost, his white-eyed gaze darting around, looking for something, anything that would explain where he was and what happened.

As he came closer, his muttering became clearer. "Still looking for night. Night was supposed to be all right…"

The ghost moved past them, hunting the empty garage for something, Emma guessed. Deluded or confused or in denial, but clearly of no help to them. Particularly considering that Emma couldn't exactly question a ghost while in the company of a detective and ERT tech.

The tech headed back to Horowitz, who'd just closed a laptop.

Mia gestured back at the victim. "Anything else? Did the unsub leave anything?"

"We've got the bullet that took off his ear and part of his head." Horowitz waved them to the small evidence table set up against the wall, where he picked up two evidence bags and displayed them for them. "These look like thirty-eight caliber rounds, full metal jacket. One went in through the back of his head above the ear and came out the other side. His vest couldn't protect his ear or head. Tech recovered the bullet from inside the brain matter on the floor, first thing."

Horowitz held the bullets in their plastic bags, angling

them so they could better examine the contents. Emma narrowed her eyes at both rounds. A .38, as common a caliber as that, would make tracing the weapon that fired it a challenge.

"The other bullet came from the shoulder of his vest. We'll run it for ballistics, but it looks like a normal .38, and you'll probably get just as much information on the weapon from using that video I sent you. It's in your inbox, by the way."

"Why didn't he radio for help?" Mia nodded to the police radio in another evidence bag. "That's working?"

Horowitz nodded. "Yeah, we checked it out. Works fine. Darby had his gun out, but why he didn't radio for help, I can't tell you."

"Panic?" Emma grimaced, disliking the answer even as she suggested it. "But if he had his gun out…I don't know. He was taken by surprise. Who wouldn't be?"

Mia shook her head. "He had to choose between his gun or the radio."

It was the right call under the circumstances. He'd just trusted a little too much and reacted a little too late.

Emma stepped back with a sigh as the medical examiner's team came through the vehicle entrance. They'd have him out of there soon.

They said their goodbyes to Detective Horowitz and the tech.

On their way out, Mia turned to Emma and lowered her voice. "I saw it in your expression. Something happened back there. You see Darby?"

Nobody was around, so Emma filled her in just as her throat tightened with the cold of the Other. She looked around. It was just Darby coming back for another circuit of the garage, still muttering about the night and how it was supposed to be all right. She gave him only a glance before nodding at the entrance.

They'd get back to the SUV, then she'd tell the rest of their team the bad news.

It looked like their unsub was pretending to be one of their own.

Or, worse, he actually was one of them.

# 5

Leo stepped out of the elevator and into the familiar chaos of the Eighth District's bullpen. Phones ringing, voices raised, chairs squeaking. All of it exactly as he remembered—except it now felt heavier.

"Didn't think we'd be back so soon." He rolled his neck, bracing for what was to come.

Vance scanned the room with a frown that made his battered face look worse. "Out of all the damn precincts in the city…what are the odds."

An officer passed, slowing when she recognized them. "Agents Jessup. Ambrose. Wish I could say it was good to see you."

*Ditto.*

Vance stuck out his hand. "Likewise, Officer Gidney."

Their phones buzzed simultaneously, and Leo hoped it'd be a "we caught our unsub" message. From the look on Vance's face as he skimmed the text, no such luck.

He nodded to Leo to follow him. "Excuse us."

"Sure thing." Officer Gidney gave a half salute and kept walking.

Vance angled toward a side window and tapped a file Emma had sent. Leo's gut clenched as a man in an FBI windbreaker extended his arm and fired his weapon. The FBI hat shadowed the man's face. Leo held his breath, silently willing him to look up. He didn't.

*Shit.*

Vance let out a breath and tucked his phone away.

Leo moved toward a quieter corner. "Tell me that's not one of ours."

"Could be, or someone playing dress-up." Vance flicked a finger at the insignia on his jacket. "These aren't exactly made of unicorn hair. Anyone determined enough could get their hands on one."

From across the room, Chief Brooks Ebenstein waved them toward his office, and Leo led the way. Ebenstein had been cooperative and congenial during their last case, when a body was dropped near the Eighth. Most of their discussions had been brief and via telephone while logistics were coordinated within the Eighth Precinct's boundaries.

"Didn't expect to work with you again so soon, but at least my people are already used to you." The chief rubbed his glasses on his shirt before shaking their hands. "I was wondering if the Bureau would send a different team. Come on in."

Leo closed the office door behind them and dropped into one of the chairs across from the chief. The older man's eyes were red, and he swept some used tissues off the desk into a garbage can. "We're all very sorry for your loss."

"Just got off the phone with Darby's mom." Ebenstein rolled his shoulders, almost like he was attempting to shove the weight of that conversation off him. "She lives in Dallas and has to fly in. Not an easy call, as you can imagine."

"I'm sure it wasn't." Leo pulled out his tablet, giving the chief a second to finish collecting himself. "From everything

I've read about Greg Darby, his loss will be strongly felt by everyone."

"Anything you could tell us about him might help." Vance glanced back through the glass door as a shout of frustration sounded out in the bullpen. "I'm sure we met him when we were here, but I'm afraid I don't remember."

"No reason to. It'll have to be quick, but I'll tell you what I can. We're already short-staffed, and now to lose a good officer like Darby…" The chief sighed. "Well. I appreciate your help. I'm hoping the man who killed him is an impostor, not an agent, but either way, I'll trust you to find him. You'd better bet my force will be doing all we can to help too."

Leo wouldn't have expected anything less. "We'll take the help, I promise. But let's start with your officer."

"Darby was well liked. And respected, too, especially considering his age and that he'd only been on the force for a year." Ebenstein half smiled. "Most guys his age have to deal with ribbing about not knowing the pecking order. Stupid jokes like being told to go pick up dry cleaning or walk a dog for an established detective. Not Darby. He had it together from the start…acted like he fit in from day one on the job."

Leo nodded, hoping for more. "Lots of friends on the force?"

"Yeah, Darby was a friendly guy. Never did anyone any harm." The chief rubbed the side of his face. "Truth is, we couldn't have lost a better rookie. Even when he was on a shit shift full of nothing but drunks, DUIs, and domestics, he took everything he did seriously. Didn't matter if he was helping a bouncer clear up a bar fight or writing a report on a kid caught shoplifting. He was diligent about the details… hell, he was a good influence. Even made some of the older guys clean up their act, if you can believe that. Reminded 'em why they're on the job."

*No wonder Ebenstein looks like he might be sick.*

"Was this one time…" Ebenstein chuckled, shaking his head. "I'll never forget it. Lady came in here panicking about how her dog was stolen. When they found out it was a mutt, few of the cops on duty started laughing her off. Greg, though? No, Greg was about to get off shift, and he went home with her to look for it. Promised he'd write up a long report if they didn't find it and catch the thief."

*Dammit. Why does shit like this always happen to the good ones?*

"What happened?"

"Greg spent all day helping that woman out. Drove all over with her. When they gave up on finding the mutt, they went back to her house so he could drop her off and get all the details for his report." The chief barked a loud, sudden laugh. "You know dogs. The mutt was sleeping on the front porch, waiting for his dinner. I'd say Greg got all of three hours' sleep that day before he was back on shift, but he said it was worth it to ease that woman's peace of mind. 'What we're here for,' I remember him telling everyone."

"Sounds like a really good guy." Vance clamped his hands on his knees. "Not someone to get in real trouble on or off the job?"

The chief shook his head, still looking a bit lost in the memory he'd just relayed.

Leo hated to press the matter but had no choice. "I know he was a rookie and probably wasn't working any big cases, but do you know if he had any contact with the Bureau? Or if there's been any conflicts between the PD and the Bureau, your precinct or any other? The FBI's got so many subdivisions, we might not know."

Leo's phone buzzed. It was Jacinda. They were needed back at headquarters, which was odd. But he had to wrap this up.

Vance also checked his text and gave him a knowing look.

Ebenstein scratched his ear. "You know the chest-thumping that Hollywood shows off between the police and FBI is mostly made up, just as well as I do. Before you guys, I couldn't tell you the last time we had an agent in here for any reason except to pick up some evidence from the locker. I don't think Darby or anyone else here had any bones to pick with the Bureau or vice versa. I wouldn't know about other precincts, but…"

Leo closed his tablet cover when the police chief went silent again. "I'd like a list of Darby's recent arrests, say for the last two months, and we may want to ask your officers some questions. Any problem with that?"

"Anything you need." He reached across to take Leo's card. "I've probably still got your other one somewhere around here. We'll get you that list of arrests today, but like I said, we're talking bar fights and a few domestics. Public drunks and DUIs. That sort of thing. But you just tell us how we can help catch the bastard who took down Greg, and we'll be on it."

Standing up, Vance led the way back out of the chief's office, picking the conversation up where they'd left off. "I bet we're dealing with some new flavor of asshole with a vendetta against cops and Feds both."

"Sounds familiar." Leo sighed. "Hard to think of a better way to ruin our rep than making it look like we've got a rogue agent attacking other law enforcement." He shifted gears. "I wonder what Jacinda wants."

Vance snorted. "Maybe one of Emma's ghosts solved the case."

Leo counted to three before responding. Getting frustrated with Vance wouldn't help right now. "You've got to let that go."

"Fine." Vance shifted on his feet, leaning back against the

window at their backs. "But, barring that, we can't ignore the possibility that this *is* actually a rogue agent. If there's one thing I've learned about the FBI lately, it's that some of us *really* know how to keep a fucking secret."

Leo stared at Vance, the venom from the other man's words coating the air.

Vance didn't flinch from his gaze. "It's the truth, isn't it?"

Swallowing, Leo finally forced himself to nod. The man had a point.

**6**

My burner vibrated in my pocket, but I ignored the damn thing. She wanted updates, but that was too bad, so sad. For once, she'd have to wait. I was operating on little sleep and needed to focus.

Officer Greg Darby had taken up most of my last few nights. Even knowing his schedule, it'd been a gamble—that he'd be near enough to the Feds' garage to pull this off. I'd practically kissed the ground when he pulled up to the curb and actually parked.

The ruse of helping carry evidence boxes felt like a thin thread, ready to snap. But Darby, ever the Boy Scout, came along with only a few questions. I wasn't surprised at his willingness to help. To a fault, Darby did the right thing. Whether it was helping little old ladies with their pets or causing headaches for local gangs.

And that was what got him in this bind in the first place.

You didn't go against family—not your given family and not the one you chose. A lot of people were learning that lesson the hard way these days.

Darby, for his short time on the police force, had always been a pain in my ass.

The burner vibrated again. This time, I reached into my pocket and rejected the call.

Sometimes, she could be so damn needy.

Since her mother died, Lydia was even more high-maintenance than usual. At least, for my support. She needed constant reassurance.

*"What about this?"*

*"What about that?"*

*"Do you think this will work?"*

*"What are the holes in the plan?"*

Honestly, Lydia was feeling pretty one-note to me lately —and she was selling herself short.

She'd managed to gather a quite comprehensive group of helpers to assist her in hunting down FBI Special Agent Emma Last, thanks to yours truly. That last guy hadn't worked out, which had sent her spiraling, but I got my baby girl back on track.

And now we were on to plan B.

Which suited me just fine, because it would help me even up some scores while simultaneously satisfying her. Win-win.

Darby—*check*!

I headed down the street toward work and debated turning my phone off before finally deciding I should answer her. If only to get her off my back for a little bit.

Leaning against the corner of a brick building, I pulled the phone out and called her.

"It's about damn time."

"I missed you, too, baby girl."

She didn't seem pleased with the term of endearment. "Don't 'baby girl' me. You've been dodging my calls."

I smiled at a man passing by on the sidewalk. He ignored me. Rude. "I've been working."

"Your *work* is all over the news."

"Of course it is. Tragedies like that always get attention." It was true. Cops' deaths were always widely discussed. There'd probably be some kind of parade for Boy Scout Darby in the coming week or so too.

Lydia's mom was denied that kind of respectful farewell. It was a point of bitter contention for her. Another thing Emma Last took. While I understood her anger, I wasn't about to point out that her mother, Detective Celeste Foss, was robbing her own police precinct for years, and that she'd been on the take. Any level of corruption she could get away with…she did. Not exactly honors material.

But I'd been with Lydia too long to do anything but agree with her.

"You left evidence behind."

I had indeed.

"Ballistics. They'll track the gun and the bullets back to my mom."

"We discussed this." It was true. I hadn't policed my brass and hoped I did the right thing. "Hundreds of weapons have been missing for years. They won't trace this back to us. Except Last. She might, and that was the point. Up her paranoia. You're welcome."

I heard her take a deep breath, gearing up to rip my ass.

I cut her off. "Look. The first domino in this plan's been tipped over. You're brilliant. You've come up with a clever way of screwing Emma Last and her people. Let's play this out."

It wouldn't matter. Foss'd been so corrupt that it wouldn't surprise anyone if she'd sold the arsenal she stolen from the Salem PD armory on the black market. But I couldn't tell

Lydia the obvious. Stroking her massive ego that I loved so much was the stronger move.

She released that deep breath in a long stream. I'd gotten through to her, and in less than five minutes. Probably a new record.

"Fine. But be careful. You're no good to me dead."

"No screwups. Now let's get ready to go knock the next domino down."

# 7

Emma crossed her legs in an attempt to stop jiggling her knee against the underside of the conference table—a physical reaction to her level of annoyance. Why they'd come back in for a briefing, she had no idea. What was the point if they hadn't learned anything yet?

At least Leo and Vance had gotten a chance to meet with Chief Ebenstein. Emma had very little to add to this emergency powwow this early in the investigation. They'd been pulled away from the crime scene before even interviewing their only witness.

The whole situation made her uneasy. The idea that a killer might be lurking within the FBI, right under their noses, and working alongside them for God knew how long? Nothing could have been more disturbing than that.

Agents were supposed to have each other's backs, and while they were obviously supposed to support every other government agency as well as police departments, Emma had always considered the bond of the Bureau something that ran a touch deeper. She didn't like comparing the camaraderie she'd felt with agents to what men and women experienced in the military, but it was closer to that than not. Fellow agents were supposed to be family, not criminals.

*Family.*

The word echoed in her mind as she looked around the conference room.

Jacinda nodded for Leo to continue talking.

He only shrugged. "That's it, Jacinda. Sorry. We talked to Chief Ebenstein and some of the cops there, but Greg Darby was well liked and had no contact with the Bureau as far as anyone knows. Family doesn't know anything either. And I've already reviewed Darby's recent arrests. The most violent offender was a drunk who tried to take Darby down with a sucker punch. Not exactly a seasoned killer, and the guy's in jail now anyway. He earned a warrant after he threw a bowling ball through some drywall at the Five Lanes Alley across town."

Vance shook his head in disgust, but then he flinched and rubbed his bruised jaw. "Talk about anger management. But it's like Leo said. The station didn't give us anything to go on, besides reminding us how recently we were there. We really think this is a coincidence?"

Emma perked up, sitting straighter. "You have something to suggest otherwise?"

"No." Leo's flat answer was the equivalent of a pitcher of cold water to the face.

Emma sat back in her seat and looked at Jacinda, who nodded for her to go next.

"Other than the video, there's not much to go on until we hear from ballistics on the thirty-eight found in Darby's brain matter." Emma pointed up to the screen, where the footage was frozen on the agent raising his gun against their stunned cop. "And the only other security camera we found was the bail bond business, but it didn't catch anything at all because of how it's angled. That's what we've got."

Mia caught her eye, lips pursed, and Emma knew she was thinking about Darby's ghost. Talking about that stuff would only chance setting Vance's anger button off again, and the spirit didn't provide any big clue to work from anyway.

"Our witness did say," Mia sat forward, facing Jacinda, "that Darby and the killer were interacting calmly. There's no way to tell whether they knew each other, but our killer didn't have to force him into that alley, and they didn't take off at a run like Darby was being lured there by some made-up emergency."

Emma leaned forward, elbows on the table. "And to be clear, the witness didn't actually know that the FBI agent killed Darby. He only knew that the cops came around this morning asking about the officer who'd died, and he ID'd Darby as the cop he'd seen talking to an FBI agent. He also didn't hear a gunshot. For all he knows, the cop stayed back there while the agent left, and someone else came in to kill him."

Mia nodded. "But we know otherwise, obviously."

"It's a start, at least." Jacinda drummed her finger along the table, nodding to herself. "I'm sure you're all wondering why I called you back here so soon. The boys upstairs have seen fit to send another agent to help with the investigation."

The room went silent, and Emma stared at Jacinda in hopes that she'd misheard her. "With everything going on..."

"That's exactly the point, Emma." Jacinda sighed and pushed herself up from the table. She went to the conference room door and waved toward her office.

The agent was there, lingering in the doorway. He must've been inside with her when they'd all filed back into the VCU, possibly waiting in Jacinda's office. And now he was heading right into the conference room.

After escorting him inside, Jacinda turned back to face

them. "Everyone, meet Special Agent Colton Wright. He'll be with us for the duration of the case."

He nodded at each of them, meeting everyone's gaze in turn. He was younger than anyone else in the room—in his late twenties, Emma guessed—but appeared professional. Dark-blond hair cut short and chiseled features, like he might've stepped out of a nighttime drama. The man was pointedly good-looking.

"Like SSA Hollingsworth said, I'm just here to help. It's nice to meet all of you. I was supposed to be here weeks ago, to fill in the gap left by Agent Monroe's injuries."

Leo's face went tight, his eyes hooded, but Emma didn't think Colton, or anyone else, noticed.

"I just had to close some other cases before the higher-ups could get me here."

Emma searched for a lie, but the explanation sounded sincere. She was irked, though. Denae had been gone a month. Why was Colton Wright showing up today? They didn't have time to deal with breaking in a new agent. They were swamped with two cases now—and pulled from the second for a meet and greet? It wasn't his fault, but it was hard not to aim her frustration in his direction.

She met Leo's eyes, and his thin-lipped smile told her he was thinking the same thing. That their new addition might be there to keep tabs on them just as much as anything. And that wasn't even mentioning the weight of trauma he was carrying around after the way things stalled out with Denae…being reminded of her like this couldn't be welcome, even if he was doing a bang-up job of hiding it.

"Now," Jacinda moved back to her seat, waving at Colton to join the table, "I want all of you to treat Agent Wright like one of the team. First things first, we need to figure out if this killer is actually an agent, and if so, who they are and why they did this. I've been on the phone with department heads all day, and I'm getting back to it, but so far, every agent's accounted for. But this case has top priority. You all catch up Agent Wright with everything you know over lunch, then I'll get you back in the field. Leo and Vance, check on ballistics. Emma and Mia, go interview that witness and canvass the area. Colton, you can go with—"

"I could do a deep dive on Darby."

"Sure, that works. I've ordered pizza, and it'll be here any minute. You're welcome." Jacinda rose from the table and left.

Emma forced herself to smile at Colton Wright, but she didn't allow herself to linger on the exchange. Whatever his brown eyes were studying, she didn't want to arouse any more suspicion, or pull his attention, if she could possibly help it.

*Maybe even close this case before the Other gets a chance to pop up again. Otherwise, it looks like we're back to keeping secrets within the team.*

And that had gone *so well* last time.

# 8

After lunch, Emma took a deep breath when she noticed Agent Colton Wright heading straight for her and Mia's desks.

Standing as he reached them, she shouldered her bag. "Agent Wright, Mia and I were just about to go interview the bail bond dealer. Our only witness from this—"

"I just wanted to touch base on a few things first. Questions come along with the first day on a new team and assignment, right?" He smiled in the way he had earlier—all charm.

Emma deflated. She didn't have time for this right now.

"If that wouldn't be too much trouble, Agent Last? And then we can all move forward on the same page, and I think things will go a lot more smoothly. Maybe I can even join you and work on looking into Darby later tonight."

*Right, because that's exactly what we were hoping for.*

Mia perched at the edge of the desk, waiting for Emma's cue.

She finally gave it. "I guess I have some questions for you also. So, yes, let's talk. Should we all sit down?"

Colton shook his head, that smile growing larger. "I don't think that'll be necessary. So…"

"How about I start?" Emma rested her bag on her desk chair, making sure to hold his gaze. "I'd love to hear more about you and your history with the FBI. It seems you know something of our team, but we only know your name."

Colton's smile remained in place, stagnant. "I'm not at liberty to discuss my history with the Bureau, I'm afraid. It's mostly classified. I'm sure you can understand something being classified?" He raised an eyebrow that felt as if it were directed at Emma and Emma alone.

Her stomach flip-flopped. She absolutely understood about secrets.

"And I really appreciate you all filling me in on the current case, but I feel like I need to back up just a bit. What can you tell me about the man you caught in the course of your last case, Hank Barnaby?"

Mia grimaced. "Do we really have time for this? It's all in the reports if you want to look them up."

Colton straightened, as if about to repeat his question or give some long defense for his curiosity.

But Emma caved and began. "Hank Barnaby." She pursed her lips, considering the question. There weren't many answers available—standard or otherwise—when it came to their most recent case. "We were pursuing various leads after Agent Vance Jessup was kidnapped. Barnaby was one of them. In questioning his neighbors, we heard something in his apartment and found Vance bound and gagged on the floor, confirming our suspicions. After that, it was a matter of determining his next target and spreading out 'til we found him. Everything was by the book."

Colton crossed his arms, those damnable eyebrows still knit, as if he were cross-examining a killer. "And what about the emails? And the money? Who funded him to attack gang members and drop their bodies where FBI and police would notice them? Who helped him kidnap Agent Jessup?"

Emma shrugged. The team had no need to hide anything now. "You know about as much as we do. I can tell you that I met with Agent Renee Bailey early this morning. She's a specialist in forensic linguistics, syntax and all that. So far, she hasn't come up with much that might help us track the emailer down, who might've funded him, but since Hank Barnaby isn't alive to talk, the messages are the main evidence we've got to go on."

"Barnaby did have a photo of Emma in his apartment. He'd written her full name on the back. The handwriting was confirmed with that in his journals." Mia looked at Emma and shrugged.

Emma hadn't intentionally left that out—maybe subconsciously, though. "Jacinda wants us sticking together. Thinks we, or I, may be being targeted because of that."

Colton's posture remained rigid, but that enigmatic smile flashed back to his face, and he showed a sliver of perfect teeth as he spoke. "And you'll update me if you hear anything else?"

"I thought you were part of the team?" Emma settled her own arms over her chest, mirroring his stance. "We all naturally update the team whenever there's something to give an update on. If you're saying you need separate updates…?"

Mia stepped forward, getting closer to Colton than Emma. "What are you doing here, exactly, Agent Wright? Are you here to help or question us?"

His smile disappeared, and his arms dropped from his chest. With a quick glance between them, he stepped back. "Excuse me, ladies. I need to make a phone call. Give me five minutes." Not bothering to wait for an answer, he made a beeline for the breakroom and shut the door behind him.

Emma sighed and was unsurprised when she watched Leo and Vance rise from the conference table and come over to meet them. She settled her bag back on her shoulder but waited.

Leo nodded at the breakroom door. "What was that about?"

"The third degree." Mia scoffed.

Vance's eyes widened a touch. "Him giving you the third degree or vice versa?"

Mia huffed at the accusation, but it came off more like she was feigning being offended.

"We weren't *not* hard on him, but he did rub us the wrong way." Emma explained as briefly as she could exactly what they'd talked about, and that Colton Wright felt more like a hall monitor checking in on a student he expected to misbehave than a new team member.

"I don't trust him either." Leo ran a hand through his hair. "Him showing up on the same day an agent gets implicated in a murder? And refusing to tell us anything about himself?"

Vance gave a quick glance to the desk Jacinda had assigned to Colton, then turned back to the group. "It's obvious he's hiding something. We have to find out what."

Mia muttered under her breath.

Vance looked at her. "What did you say?"

"What did I say?" Mia stared at him hard, and Emma suddenly wished she could disappear. "I *said* that not everyone is hiding something from you. I agree the guy's an ass, but that doesn't mean he's keeping secrets we need to start focusing on."

*Shit. That was pointed.*

Vance's cheeks went a touch red, but Leo was already talking before he could respond.

"Look, we've all got our doubts, but that's all they are, and we've all been the new guy." He turned and strode back toward the conference room as if the conversation were closed, and Vance followed him after meeting Mia's eyes for a few seconds.

When he'd shut the conference room door behind him, though, Emma turned to Mia. "You okay?"

She shook her head. "I'm fine. Vance is just so…so *not*. Lately, I mean."

Emma knew exactly what she meant. Vance had been almost unbearably suspicious and moody ever since he learned that she had paranormal abilities. Not that she could blame him, not really. But it seemed that he was letting that bit of news overshadow all the good that ever came between them as friends and colleagues.

It hurt that the rest of her didn't matter. Everything they'd been through, every case, every late-night debrief over takeout, every time they'd had each other's backs in the field —it all felt like it had been wiped clean by one truth she never asked for and had no control over.

He looked at her now like he didn't recognize what he saw. Like she was some stranger who'd infiltrated his team.

And maybe she got it. Kind of.

She might've felt the same way if the roles were reversed. If someone she trusted suddenly turned into something *other*. Something that didn't fit in the world they built their careers on.

Still, it didn't make the distance easier to stomach.

"I think he's trying." She glanced at his back. "He just doesn't know what to do with the version of me that doesn't make sense."

Mia gave her a soft look but didn't speak. She didn't have to.

Emma grabbed her bag and headed toward the elevator. "He'll come around. Or he won't." Her throat was tight with guilt. "I'm sorry, Mia."

Mia gripped her elbow lightly as they stepped into the elevator without Agent Wright. "This isn't your fault. It's obvious he was always capable of turning into Mr. Doom and Gloom, and it just happened to come around now. We'll either get past it or we won't, I guess. But one way or another, I'm not putting up with his paranoia throwing our whole team off-track or putting a hitch in my step."

Mia's own pessimism and snark wasn't exactly Mia-like. Not any more than Vance's new attitude was vintage Vance. But Emma didn't dare say that.

**9**

Leo stared at his partner's retreating back. "Where're you going?"

Vance only cursed and marched toward Jacinda's office.

They were supposed to be going to the lab. Check on that .38 found at the crime scene. If they could link the ballistics from the recovered bullet to a gun, they'd be getting somewhere, even if it turned out to be a weapon registered to someone in the FBI.

Leo likewise pivoted and followed his heated colleague, thankful, at least, to see Vance bothering to knock on Jacinda's door rather than just bursting in.

"Jacinda." Vance spoke low. "You said everyone was being looked into, but our newest buddy, Colton Wright, didn't tell us anything about himself."

Her nose wrinkled, and she leaned back in her chair. "You want to look into each other now? Why do you need his file? He doesn't have either of your files."

Leo stepped in beside Vance. "Come on, Jacinda. Isn't it a little strange for someone to join our team at exactly this moment? We're just trying to cover our bases and be smart here."

"All right, hold on. It should be here anyway." She turned back to her monitor and typed. "I requested files for all nonsupervisory special agents in this field office. His should be here somewhere…"

As she clicked and frowned, Vance perched in the chair across from her and leaned forward. "It's not there."

She shook her head. "No, you're right. It's not. Probably because he's on the team, his transfer was already in the works before Darby was killed. I'll have to send another request and just ask for his file specifically. We'll get there. Meanwhile…"

"No 'meanwhile,' Jacinda, please." Vance lowered his voice at the sharp look she gave him, and Leo stepped all the way inside her office and closed the door behind him. "This is serious."

Jacinda ignored him and began typing. When she looked up, she waved at her computer. "It's done, all right? Get back to work. Let this go."

"What Vance is saying so non-diplomatically," Leo made sure to keep his voice a smidge more even than his partner's, "is that this feels super suspicious. Files aside, him showing up right this second is hard to ignore, ya know?"

Jacinda brushed some of her hair back from her face as she looked between them. "I've got no doubt that he's just here to offer support, and you two knuckleheads are more focused on circling the wagons than letting him help. That's what I'm seeing."

Jacinda sounded just like Yaya, and Leo felt himself wilting instead. Maybe they were being paranoid. Maybe they were being bullies to the new kid on the playground, though Leo never really thought of himself that way.

"And maybe it's not surprising," Jacinda went on, "because lots of people in the FBI are suspicious of this VCU right now because of what happened with the Salem situation. There are a lot of questions around why D.C. agents were in Massachusetts at all. If management sent Colton here because they trust him and want to make sure they can trust us, too, so be it. We should welcome him with open arms so maybe we can put that whole mess behind us as fast as possible."

Vance rubbed at the butterfly bandage on his head. "It's not that simple. If he'd showed up last week, sure, but he showed up today. A cop turns up dead, and we find out it was an agent, and video confirms it, and you don't think we should be looking into the new face?"

"He fits the build." Leo then surprised himself by adding, "Like the rest of us."

Jacinda stared at the two of them. "He didn't show up on his own. The man is a special agent with the FBI. I got an email from the higher-ups telling me to expect him, and even if you don't trust my email or his badge, you've got to trust me when I tell you that I saw his supervisor in person today. Colton can't be an impostor if he has a supervisor I know, a badge, and experience, and he was assigned to our team, as I stated, before Greg Darby was killed."

Vance sat back in his seat with an unapologetic grimace.

"Guys, tamp down your paranoia about Colton and focus on the case, okay?" Jacinda met Leo's gaze, nodding back toward the conference room. "We've all got our work to do, just like Colton has his. If he's here to watch us on this case, so be it. That means the sooner it's over, the sooner he'll move on to his next assignment."

Leo was about to agree when Jacinda's phone rang.

She held up one hand to quiet them. "SSA Jacinda Hollingsworth...yes, sir." She pursed her lips, listening. "I understand, sir. Of course. We're on it."

Leo shared a look with Vance. This didn't sound promising.

When Jacinda hung up, she wore a mask of concern. "That seals the question. My request for Colton's file has officially been denied. We are to focus our efforts on the task at hand, eliminating possibilities from our suspect pool. Is that understood?"

Vance slammed himself to his feet and left the office.

Leo looked at Jacinda and nodded. "Understood."

For now, Colton Wright was part of their team and had to be trusted—even if his file was off-limits.

# 10

The bail bond business had a neon *Always Open* sign flashing in the window, and Emma braced herself for a seedy, shag-carpeted interior. Instead, the scent of lemongrass greeted her when she pulled open the door. Incense smoke drifted up from two little brown cones set up on the corner of a large right-angle desk with papers and folders strewn across one side. A computer monitor and open area faced the room and door.

A man behind the behemoth piece of furniture glanced up and waved them in. "Come on, come on. Not like I haven't been waiting here all day on you. Name's Louis Robinson. I own this place." He pushed one hand through frizzy, mousy-brown hair, giving the impression of a tired journalist more than the sleazy lawyer type Emma expected. "You find your killer FBI agent yet? I was hoping that was the holdup."

Emma inwardly cringed but didn't take the bait.

"No." She sat down across from him, perching on the edge of a hard plastic seat. "But that's why we're here. I'm Special Agent Emma Last, and this is Special Agent Mia

Logan. We understand you saw the officer leave his vehicle this morning?"

"And I told the cops everything, but they still asked me to stick around for you. Sent my morning guy out to get us breakfast, since I had to be here. And now he's out there scrounging up some lunch. Been up for over twenty-four hours now, and I'm tihangry."

Emma cocked her head, puzzling the new word together. "Tired, hungry…and angry."

"So you're as smart as you look." The bail bond dealer cracked an unexpected smile. It was gone in a flash, but they'd seen it.

Mia raised an eyebrow. "You always work overnight, even though you own this place?"

"You know how many people call here at night? I like to be the one who gets the first impression of clients. And it's easier to get work done." He pulled his incense closer, leaned in, and sniffed in some smoke directly. "This stuff's all that's keeping me awake. Normally, I'd be home in bed by now."

*Better ask him what you need to before we all get high on lemongrass, Emma girl.*

"Louis, we appreciate your time. We're hoping you don't mind sharing everything you saw one more time." He looked like he might argue, but Emma cut him off. "This is part of the process, so you'll have to bear with us if you don't want us bothering you to come down to the station, and we need to be sure you weren't involved."

"I wasn't involved!" He huffed, mussing his frizzy hair again.

Mia shot him her signature dimpled smile.

"Fine. Whatever you say, but I wasn't involved."

Emma shifted her tablet in her lap, pointedly, and he narrowed his eyes on her. But he also got the point.

Louis twined his fingers and rested his hands on his belly

as he leaned back in his chair. "Right around five this morning, I heard some shouting. Couldn't tell if it was a fight or what, so I looked outside. Saw a man in an FBI cap and windbreaker waving at a police car. Cop pulled over. Him and the FBI guy talked for a second, then the cop got out. It was Darby. We're friendly, I guess, working the graveyard shifts and all. Anyway, I could tell it was him soon as he stepped out. Two of 'em walked down the alley that goes between this strip mall and the bank, toward the parking garage."

Mia held her smile, oozing charm. "Could you describe the agent for us?"

Louis shrugged. "He was kind of tall maybe, a little thin, I guess. Cap covered his hair, but it looked pretty short. Blended in, maybe. Light skin, so I'd say he's a white guy, but I can't be sure of that. The bill of the cap put most of his face in shadow. He wasn't Black like Darby, though."

"And do you have any footage of what unfolded?" Emma gestured to the front door. "I saw your camera outside."

"I already checked." Louis typed on his phone, then held it out for Emma to see.

Only the little walkway directly in front of the business and a few inches of parking lot was in view.

"That's the only one up, and we've got it set up primarily for break-ins. Neither of those guys came close enough for it to catch their shoes, let alone faces."

Mia glanced outside, then back at Louis. "And what time did you hear the gunshots?"

*Nice one, Mia. See if he gets caught telling us something he didn't tell the cops.*

But the bail bond dealer's eyes only narrowed further. "I didn't hear any gunshots. If I had, you don't think I would've called you?" The man's indignation spilled off his words.

Emma pulled out her business card and handed it across the desk. "If you think of anything else."

"I'll call." Louis perched the card against his keyboard. "Shame about Darby," he said, mostly to himself, then looked back and forth between them pointedly. "That it?"

Emma smiled flatly. "Just expect us to be in touch if we need to discuss the matter further. Fair enough?"

The bond agent grunted something that might or might not have been agreement, waving a hand for them to go.

Back out in the parking lot, Emma gazed around the scene. Louis was their only witness. They'd been told earlier that the gas station across the way didn't have working security footage, and their counter wouldn't have been angled to see the street anyway.

"I don't know why our unsub would've been shouting." Mia stepped closer to Emma, tucking her tablet back into her bag. "Why draw attention to yourself when you're about to commit a murder?"

"He sure wasn't discreet." Emma shook her head. "I'd say that's the major clue telling us he's not actually FBI."

Mia adjusted the strap on her shoulder. "I think it's possible he could be. Though, motive-wise...I don't know. A cop got in the way of a big case he was closing? A cop let a major suspect go free and ruined months of casework? It still doesn't seem like he'd go after a random rookie if he was FBI."

Emma chewed on that notion as she led the way across the parking lot and back toward the scene. They'd take one more look, then make a pass through the neighborhood to see if anything was missed.

"It feels like the unsub has to be an impostor. No FBI agent would kill a police officer in cold blood, let alone in a way that advertised their Bureau affiliation. That wouldn't just be career suicide but a fast track to federal prison, if not the death penalty. It's absurd."

"Maybe a retired agent that wants to make the Bureau look bad. Has a beef to pick with them, maybe?" In a couple previous cases, a few law enforcement officers had seemed to grow unimpressed with the badge over time. Barnaby. A former officer named Renfield.

"He didn't move like any kind of *retired* in the footage. He was fast like Darby, who was young and agile."

"Well, then he's going after Darby specifically, and we have to find the link. But let's not forget FBI retires at fifty-seven, not exactly geriatric. Especially with our fitness requirements."

"Granted." Emma nodded. "But if he's not FBI, we're looking at a civilian killer who got his hands on an FBI jacket and cap, and he wants to make the Bureau look bad or distract us from the reason that *he*, personally, wanted Darby dead."

"But why would someone *in* the FBI wear their gear to commit murder?" Mia shook her head.

That was the million-dollar question they kept circling back to. Emma agreed the logic in that argument was thin, which brought them back to the theory that they were looking for an unhinged civilian with a god complex and a penchant for murder.

# 11

Officer Freddy Gorik's cruiser stank of grease from his late lunch. He flicked the air freshener attached to the middle vent in annoyance. The damned thing didn't do any good.

The ringing of his personal cell phone interrupted the silence, and he picked it up as he came to a stop at a light. *Screw the hands-free law.* Like he always said, that wasn't anything a cop would pull another cop over for.

He didn't recognize the number on his screen, but it was local. His dad calling from a borrowed phone because his own cell had died again, probably.

"Hello?"

Silence met his voice for a few seconds, but before he could hang up, a woman spoke, hard-edged and fast. "Hi, Freddy. I want you to listen up, because I know about the deal you took. And if you don't listen, your career's going to be over. Do we understand each other?"

Freddy yanked the steering wheel to the right, nearly pulling his cruiser up onto the curb, and shoved it in park. "I'm listening, yeah."

"Good. You're going to do whatever I tell you to, and if you don't, I'll go to the media."

Panic turned the meal he'd eaten into acid, and he took the phone away from his ear for a second to stare at the number again. Unrecognizable. This was his worst nightmare.

The deal was over. Done with. He'd played his part like a champ, taken his money, and buzzed off, just like they'd planned.

*Why now?*

"You're going to go get one thousand dollars in cash and bring it to the corner of Oak Street and Eighth Avenue, to a big gray house, southwest corner. Now. Got it?"

Freddy swallowed. "What is this—"

"This isn't the time for questions, Freddy." Her voice dripped through the line like venom.

His limbs felt numb, frozen.

"Get yourself to an ATM and do as you've been instructed."

The line going dead felt like a hammer dropping on his kneecap, but he swallowed the indignity of it. He had no choice.

"This is just about money." He dropped his phone in the cup holder beside his empty soda, put the car in drive, and pulled forward against the red light. He'd come to a gas station a few miles up. "Let's get this over with. Just get this over with."

The deal was a one-off. He'd looked the other way for some small-time smuggling operation and been rewarded for it. It'd been months ago. Nobody was supposed to have known.

At the gas station, he slammed his bank card into the ATM and removed a thousand dollars from his meager savings.

*That bitch must know what shit pay cops get, or she would've asked for more.*

It reminded him what a shit deal he had in life.

Back in the cruiser, he shoved the cash into his phone wallet, making sure to tuck it in. If anyone saw him during the handoff, they'd first notice him fiddling with his phone, and everyone and their mother spent half their lives on their phones nowadays. Nobody'd notice the handoff, cop or not.

"Eighth and Oak. Eighth and Oak." He muttered to himself as he drove, trying to place the location. Once he reached Oak Street and turned left, though, he realized why it was so unfamiliar, even though it was well within his beat. "They want to do a handoff in the fucking suburbs? What the hell is this?"

At the southwest corner, a nice-looking gray ranch-style house sat taking up a large corner lot. A big shade tree covered most of the yard in dim shadows even at midafternoon on a sunny day. He pulled to the curb and looked around. Across the street, an old woman was watering her flowers, but she was the only sign of life.

Nevertheless, he pulled himself together, set aside his frustration, and climbed out of his cruiser. He slammed the door, and was just considering whether he should go to the front door or wait for some sign when a shout caught his attention.

From the side of the house, a man in FBI clothing stepped out. "Freddy Gorik? Agent Ron Knight." The FBI agent waved, like the two of them were old friends, meeting up to watch a Nationals game over some beers.

Freddy stiffened. "What the hell?" He edged around the cruiser, squinting at the figure. "What, um, are you doing here?"

The agent didn't answer right away. He glanced over his shoulder, scanning the yard. "Who'd you expect?"

"Not a Fed." Freddy stopped walking. His gut had already started twisting. Something was off—too off.

This guy looked legit. Young, clean-cut, fit. Windbreaker crisp and everything. But the threats Freddy had gotten? The tone of that call?

Nothing about it felt right.

He hovered between the car and the tree line, half in shadow. Too close now to sprint without drawing fire, not close enough to do a damn thing if the guy made a move.

The agent made the move, a revolver coming up in a blur.

Before Freddy could even process why an FBI agent carried that style of weapon or question his intentions to use it, he ducked and dove around the corner of the house, shoulder hitting the dirt as he rolled to cover. His hand found the grip of his sidearm, pulled it free.

*Feds were listening. That has to be it. Fucking Feds were listening to my calls.*

"Agent Knight, let's talk about it!" He came up in a crouch, breath ragged, gun raised—

But the shot had already been fired.

The impact lifted Freddy, slammed him sideways against the house. All the air in his lungs vanished in an instant.

His hand flew to his throat. Warm. Wet. Sticky.

Blood.

He dropped to his knees, then collapsed, his spine scraping down the wall until he hit the concrete. Vision stuttering. Every breath harder than the last.

Across the yard, the agent ducked beneath the tree's thick canopy, his figure shrinking into shadow as he disappeared.

A car peeled out somewhere nearby.

Freddy's gun was right there, just inches away. His fingers twitched but didn't curl.

If he could still hear his heartbeat, he had to be alive.

Right?
*One...two...three...*

# 12

With the windbreaker and FBI cap under the seat and the gun tucked safely into the center console, I kept one eye focused on the speedometer as I drove. The cap over my brow now advertised the Washington Nationals, just like a gazillion other sports fans across the city.

Every instinct I had screamed at me to floor the gas pedal, but I'd already pulled away and driven off way too fast for a suburban neighborhood. I had to be cool.

A woman taking up most of the road forced me sideways even on the wide subdivision road, her mouth going a mile a minute the whole time. A little kid stared at me from the back seat as the car passed.

I should've parked farther away. Should've planned my exit strategy better. Should've thought about kindergartens and day cares letting out and adding bodies and vehicles to the streets. Adding witnesses.

*Damn traffic had me held up so long. I was supposed to get there ahead of Gorik.*

As it was, I'd only rolled up with a minute to spare before Gorik's cruiser nosed its way down the street.

At least I made it, and Lydia wouldn't bitch at me. Now I just had to get the hell out of Dodge without calling attention to myself.

The edge of the subdivision came up, and I took a hard left onto Stanley Street. Back into a real flow of cars and away from the damn school zone. A pizza delivery driver sped by, but I didn't take his cue and follow.

This was a good place to get lost in traffic. All the comings and goings might've worked against me earlier, but they were a boon now. Moving into the middle lane, I chose to tail a Tahoe. I clocked a pair of flailing arms in the back seat. Some snot-nose having a tantrum no doubt, parent focused on them.

All I had to do was keep my cool, and I'd be golden.

The Tahoe was going a perfect fifteen in a thirty because of the clogged road, and if I just followed it, I'd blend in with every other stiff grabbing their kid from day care or rushing off to fit in errands before older kids came home from school.

*But the one witness saw me, for sure. That was good.*

That lady across the street better have been able to read *FBI* written in giant yellow letters. It'd be my luck to get the one blind bat in the neighborhood.

She'd definitely heard me fire my weapon, though, and then she'd seen Gorik fall. She dropped her hose and fell all over her flowers. Hilarious. I just hoped she wasn't so old that I'd killed her along with the crooked cop. We needed her to be a witness.

"She better've called the cops."

My phone buzzed in my pocket. I rolled my eyes. "Now's not a good time."

The Tahoe slammed on its brakes, and I did the same.

"Dammit."

Last thing I needed was a car accident near the scene. I might as well have a neon arrow over my head.

People needed to learn to fucking drive.

I breathed deeper, ignoring the urge to speed into the fast lane and give the Tahoe mom the middle finger.

My phone went off again.

I answered. "Now is really not a good time."

"Is it done? That's great." She seemed pleased to have called in the middle of the action. I hated to admit it, but it turned me on to hear her happy. She covered the phone and spoke to someone nearby, then came back on the line. As if I had all the time in the world. "And did someone see?"

"A neighbor. Old lady who was out watering the lawn or some shit. I saw another woman rushing toward her, too, so she either saw me or saw the lady react." I refrained from adding that she'd fallen over and might've had a coronary.

"Your face was hidden?"

"No, I let everyone see me."

"Don't get snippy." She breathed out, audible pleasure in her voice. "Did you leave anything behind?"

She meant ballistics. "You know I did."

She sighed, sounding as content as a cat. If we were in the bedroom, I'd appreciate that little noise, and I'd get her to give me a few more. We were on the same page again. Agent Ron Knight was the killer of both cops, using a stolen weapon from the Salem PD. It got me just as hot when Lydia caved to *my* whims too. When she bent a little, understanding my motivation mattered...almost as much as hers.

I slowed the car and pulled it way right. A cop sped by, all lights and sirens, heading to good ole Freddy Gorik, no doubt. About time.

*How fucking long would you guys have taken if I hadn't*

*advertised for the old lady to call you? I should have a talk with them about their response times.*

"Remember, the day's not done yet. Are you still with me?" She pitched her voice low and seductive. I adjusted in my seat, embarrassed that such a simple shift in tone had such an effect. Probably the result of adrenaline from the rush.

"Quick stop at home, and on to the next bit of work. You got it, baby girl."

"Perfect."

She hung up.

Another cop sped by, heading to my latest kill.

**13**

Emma drove down a suburban street and stopped beneath a wide shade tree holding court on a substantial corner lot. She pulled up just behind where Vance and Leo were parked. The perpendicular street was blocked off with crime scene tape, and a couple of cops stood listening to nosy neighbors. Some of them craned their necks at cops and ambulances, and others stomped their feet about being cut off from their usual dog-walking route.

Two reporters were just getting set up for live shots on the other side of the ruckus, but that was inevitable. Between a handful of witnesses and the location of the kill, there was no way to keep this under wraps.

After unbuckling and hopping out, Mia pointed at the leaf-heavy oak in the center of their destination, its trunk tied with yellow tape. "Brings a new meaning to 'Tie a Yellow Ribbon Round the Ole Oak Tree,' doesn't it? Man, am I getting sick of seeing crime scene types blocking off the bodies of cops."

Nodding sadly, Emma climbed from the vehicle and moved up to meet Leo and Vance. The crime scene tape wrapped around the tree appeared even more garish against this neat picture of suburbia, but she tried to ignore it as she took in the scene. Beyond the tape, two ambulances were parked, one with its back doors open and an elderly woman in civilian clothes sitting inside. Her legs dangled above the ground as a paramedic examined her. Beyond that, cops hovered around the edge of the ranch-style house, whispering.

Leo pulled his cap down over his shaggy hair and moved in beside Emma as they ducked under the crime scene tape. "Before we get over there, you should know Vance and I discovered something about Colton Wright."

"It seems he's the only agent in D.C. who's so untouchable that we don't have access to his file."

Mia looked at Leo rather than addressing Vance. "What'd Jacinda say?"

Before he could answer, Vance stalked ahead, off toward the detective moving to intercept them.

"She said focus on the case." Leo waved them forward, already hurrying after Vance.

Mia groaned. "That's bullshit."

Emma nearly stumbled from surprise. Mia *never* cursed. "Hey, are you—"

"I'm fine!" Mia shot her a glare, then slowed, letting Leo move on ahead of them. Vance had already reached the detective, who Emma vaguely recognized, but she slowed to a stop to focus on Mia for a second.

"Did you see the way Vance acted? He didn't even look at me when we all met up! He just avoids everything."

Holding back from telling Mia that *she'd* also avoided looking at *him*, Emma could only shake her head. "Like Leo said, let's just focus on the case for now. We'll figure Vance out later, okay? Maybe he's just stressed that a second cop has been gunned down by a federal agent or someone wearing FBI gear. In broad daylight this time, according to the witness."

Pointedly, Emma nodded ahead to where Leo and Vance were already introducing themselves to the detective. Vance stood with his hands clasped in front of him, putting on an air of respectability even though his face looked like he'd gone four rounds with a heavyweight champ.

A little of the bluster went out of Mia's expression.

The detective was just tucking his badge away when Emma and Mia reached the men, and he nodded at the two of them. "Can't say I mind this case belonging to the Feds. What a mess. Detective Fletcher. You hear about Freddy already, I understand?"

"Freddy's our victim?" Emma softened her voice. "The two of you knew each other, then. I'm sorry for your loss."

The man was fiddling with his belt, but he stiffened at the comment. "Don't be sorry on my account. Freddy Gorik was, uh...something. Don't want to speak ill of the dead, but we weren't friends. Different senses of humor, you could say."

Vance stepped closer. "Meaning what, exactly?"

The detective's face went a touch red. "Meaning Freddy and I didn't share the same politics, okay? He was a blowhard. Didn't deserve to die. I'm not saying that. But we didn't get along. The cop we lost yesterday was a great guy, from what I hear, though I didn't know him, but if we had to lose someone else..."

Mia's jaw dropped, and the detective seemed to hear himself for the first time.

He straightened and shook his head. "I shouldn't have said anything, so forget I did. The techs collected Freddy's wallet, phone, et cetera, but I'm assuming you all want to talk to our witnesses first? This way. For what good it'll do you. Older woman's being treated for shock, and there's another neighbor who saw the cop fall but not the unsub."

Before Emma could stop him, Detective Fletcher had turned and moved off toward the closest ambulance. Following on his heels, Emma heard the elderly woman before she saw her.

"I should talk to my doctor. I must've blacked out." The gray-haired white woman shook her head hard enough to make her curls shimmy, putting one hand up to her temple. "Does that happen with things like this? Did I hallucinate?"

"Ma'am, we can take you to the hospital."

"No. I said, no. I'm fine. I'd like to phone my doctor, though. He worries about me."

Emma stepped beside the visibly exasperated paramedic. She held out her ID and badge. "Ma'am, I'm Special Agent Emma Last. Can I ask your name?"

"Linda Weller." The woman turned her sharp blue eyes back on the young paramedic beside her. "And these lovely first responders have been…lovely."

Leo offered one of his charming grins, speaking to the paramedic as much as the woman before them. "Are you injured?"

Linda didn't answer, only drew herself up and crossed her arms.

Stepping back, the paramedic echoed her posture as if they were in a schoolyard. "She checks out fine. Says she thinks she blacked out or hallucinated, so I offered to take her to the hospital, but she refused and wants to call her GP or have me get him here, which I can't do."

Emma caught the elderly woman's eyes. She was maybe in her late seventies, but she looked able. "We'll let you decide what you want to do in a few minutes, okay? Right now, could you tell us what you saw, Mrs. Weller?"

"That's the problem!" She snorted. "What I saw doesn't make sense, so I think I blacked out. Hallucinated!"

Vance snorted, and Leo shot him a quick glare before

stepping between him and the woman, stealing her focus. "Linda...can I call you Linda?"

She gave a reluctant nod.

Emma glanced at Mia to share a tiny grin over Leo working his charm, but she'd moved away to talk to some cops. Avoiding Vance, maybe.

"Linda." Leo projected calm in every syllable. "How about you just tell us what you remember? Whatever that might be?"

Linda pursed her lips, but finally she nodded. "I was out watering my tulips in the front yard. The police officer pulled up across the street and parked by the curb. That's his car there."

She waved at the black-and-white parked in front of the wide ranch-style home. Beyond it, Emma glimpsed their victim for the first time. Slouched against the front of the house with feet sticking out from under a sheet.

"He walked up to Martha Lancaster's house, even though she's at work. Got some bigwig job in AI, no kids, no man, always working. Then an FBI agent showed up like a bat out of hell from her side yard, waving like they're friends from childhood. I stopped watering because I thought it was sweet. Also, I've never seen one man at Martha's house, let alone two. In uniform, no less."

Vance stepped forward to refocus her. "And you knew he was an agent because..."

"His jacket and baseball cap looked just like yours." Linda narrowed her eyes at each of them in turn. "But I wouldn't know. My nephew says you can buy anything on eBay these days, and I've always trusted law enforcement, but today..."

Emma gritted her teeth so hard they squeaked. She forced her face to relax. "What happened next, ma'am?"

Linda swallowed hard and began rubbing her upper arms.

For the first time, Emma thought maybe they should insist she go to the emergency room.

"That's where I get confused." She tapped her temple. "The cop answered him, said something I couldn't hear. One second, it looked like they were going to shake hands, a reunion of sorts. Then the cop just froze as the agent raised his gun. The cop ran around the side of Martha's house, and I guess I should've run too, but I was also frozen. The agent ran after him, all the while the cop is yelling, 'Agent Knight, let's talk about it!' And the agent—"

Emma lifted a hand. "Did you say, 'Agent Knight?'"

"Yeah, Knight. Maybe Nile. I told you, they acted like pals at first. So the agent came back out front and went under the oak on steroids." Linda stopped and shook her head. Her breathing was growing heavier.

Leo bent his knees to meet her at eye level where she sat. "And then what, Linda? What happened?"

"I heard voices but couldn't make anything out. The FBI guy was under that tree." She scowled. "Damn tree should be illegal. You could hide an army under it. We've got an HOA. They need to do something about it." She lowered her voice, her eyes going glassy. "Before the cop could do much, the agent just…killed him. I fell on my backside when the gun went off. Right on my tulips, I was so shocked."

*Maybe she is in shock.*

"And that gun was so loud. So loud. I didn't know guns were so loud. I must've blacked out or something. And then I heard someone scream, 'Call 911!'" Panic dripped from Linda Weller's words.

Emma stepped forward as the paramedic placed one hand on her elbow. "The officer shouted for help?"

Linda turned her gaze back on Emma. "I went over and saw that officer, to see if I could help, and he was shot good.

Dead." She hesitated, and she began rubbing at her arms more briskly.

"What is it, Linda?" Leo patted her shoulder.

"I think the FBI agent is the one who yelled for me to call you people." The woman nearly whimpered after saying it but then attempted a weak smile under the paramedic's disapproving stare.

Emma caught Leo's grim gaze and then addressed Linda again. "It's possible you blacked out the middle part of what happened, maybe, because of how traumatic it was. You should talk to your doctor. Can you tell us what this agent looked like, though?"

Linda shook her head. "Tall and gangly, a bit. But everyone's tall compared to me, so I don't know. I only got a look at his profile, but didn't see anything that stood out. A white fella, if that helps. But he hid under that tree, mostly."

Emma pulled Leo aside as Vance asked a few more questions, doing what he could to confirm details. Detective Fletcher had remained nearby, observing, and now he pointed to a young Black woman with an infant hugging her shoulder. "That's the other witness, Elizabeth Soyinka."

The woman glanced away from the cop she'd been speaking to as Emma approached, her eyes doubtful. "No matter how many questions they ask me, I can't help much."

With a shrug, the cop backed off, and Leo offered his card. "Hi, Elizabeth, I'm Special Agent Leo Ambrose, and this is Special Agent Emma Last."

The woman took it between two fingers and held it against her baby's back as she bobbed him in the soothing rhythm good parents seemed to master.

"Just tell us what you can."

Emma nodded assurance when the woman's dark-brown eyes came back to hers, and that seemed to steady her, though Emma had already noticed she was keeping her back to the house. Didn't want to witness the body again, she guessed.

"I saw Linda fall." She gestured with her chin to somewhere behind her. "I live two houses down and was just pulling in and getting Miles out of his car seat. I heard a loud bang and saw her fall in her flower bed. I thought…"

The woman's face crumpled as she breathed more heavily, joggling her baby a touch faster. When he whimpered, she made an apologetic murmur to him and slowed down.

"I thought…thought Linda'd been shot. And my husband would kill me, God bless him, but I left Miles in his seat and ran to her. She was getting up when I reached her, then she went across the street. I watched her, but…" Elizabeth shook her head, tears starting to slip from her eyes.

"It's okay. You're doing great, Elizabeth. Take your time."

"I saw that officer on the ground, and I knew. I knew he had to be dead from the angle he was at. I just stayed and waited for Linda to come back after she checked on him. I was a coward. And then I went to get Miles, and we called 911 and waited until the paramedics and cops showed up."

Emma leaned down so that the woman couldn't avoid her eyes. "Elizabeth, you were *not* a coward. I'd never advise someone to run out into the open when they hear a gunshot, but your first thought was for your neighbor. That's not cowardly behavior. And keeping your baby in the safety of the car was the right thing to do."

A little whimper came from the woman's throat, but she finally nodded. "Is Linda okay?"

Leo stepped aside so Elizabeth could better view the ambulance and her neighbor. "She's fine. Struggling with what she saw, which is natural. Trying to bully the paramedic into getting her GP to do a house call."

Elizabeth's lips quirked. "That does sound like Linda.

Don't tell her ambulances cost money either. She can afford the ride but won't want to."

"Oh, she's refusing to go to the hospital." Emma waved at the baby as the woman turned him in her arms, cradling him. "Elizabeth, what can you tell us about the shooter?"

Her gaze lifted from her baby, meeting Emma's in surprise. "The shooter? Nothing."

Leo frowned. "You mean it happened too fast, or…"

Elizabeth shook her head. "I'm sorry, but I didn't see him. I saw Linda fall, and I was so focused on her…I just ran to her. Maybe I saw a blur out of the corner of my eye, but honestly, that's probably just me imagining it because the cops over there insist that I must've seen something." The woman scoffed, shooting the nearby cops an annoyed look.

Emma glanced at them, then off toward the woman's vehicle. Its side door still hung open, proving it was hers. There was no telling if her line of sight would've been blocked by trees or vehicles, but even so…if she'd been focused on Linda, she might well have had tunnel vision and not processed anything but the older woman falling. "Did you hear the officer tell Linda to call 911?"

"I heard someone scream it. I can't imagine it could've been the dead officer. It carried strength and volume. It was a man's voice, that's all I can tell you."

"If you happen to remember anything…" Emma tucked her card next to Leo's between two of Elizabeth's fingers.

The mother nodded. "I'll call. I promise."

Leo cooed some unintelligible sounds at the baby, making Elizabeth smile.

Then she spoke up again. "I feel like this is unrelated, but I saw a car speed off in the distance, you know, behind the house."

"Can you describe the car?"

"Yeah, actually, because I owned one just like it. It was my first college car. An old Toyota RAV4 from the early 2000s, dark green, just like mine was."

Leo jotted it all down. "I can't imagine—"

"Too far away for the license plate. Not sure I would've thought to memorize it anyway."

"Elizabeth. Thank you. This is very helpful. You have our cards."

The two of them excused themselves and headed toward the crime scene. They stopped near the middle of the street, both taking in the panorama of the scene.

Leo waved at a figure hurrying toward them—Agent Colton Wright.

Still pulling his jacket on, Colton stopped directly in front of them with a frazzled demeanor. Static electricity from the jacket sent tiny strands of his hair sticking up. "Catch me up?"

Unable to hold back sarcasm, Emma pulled her phone from her pocket and held it up for the other agent's viewing. "Didn't you get the same text the rest of us did?"

Colton's lips tightened. "I got here as fast as I could. I would've been with you, had you and Agent Logan not left without me."

Emma couldn't argue that point.

"Have you already spoken to the witnesses?"

Leo nodded. "Yeah, at length."

"And?" Colton glanced back and forth between them, then off toward Vance. "Did they see the supposed agent?" His eyes widened a touch.

Leo gave Colton the abridged version.

Emma stood there quietly, working on keeping her face neutral. She had no legitimate reason to be irked with Colton. Did she like that an agent was hired to likely spy on them? No, but file or no file, she didn't think he was their killer. That would've been too easy. No, he was just a jerk sent to be their big brother and watch their every move, and to some end, she got that.

Looking over toward the body, Emma zeroed in on Mia standing with an ERT tech. "I think I'll go catch up with Logan, and we'll check out the victim. You two see if you can find any more witnesses?"

Vance nodded agreement. "Fine by me." He turned and stalked toward the lookie-loos being held back by crime scene tape.

Leo and Emma watched him go. "And as much as we'd hate to admit it…"

Emma nodded. "My thinking too. We'll get more done if Vance and Mia aren't on the same task."

Meanwhile, her focus went to Colton, who'd moved over toward the body with the cop he'd left to question.

Serving as mediator between the Other and her own reality and between Mia and Vance was all hard enough. Emma no longer felt sure she was up for navigating this new ground with Colton Wright in the mix.

And since her own little quirk was at the center of what they needed to keep hidden, that could only spell disaster for her sooner or later.

# 14

Emma found Mia peering down at the body of their fallen officer.

Freddy Gorik lay sprawled on the lawn, his uniform soaked in blood, a deep, spreading bloom over his chest. His eyes—wide, glassy—locked on the sky as if it held answers he'd never get.

Maybe questioning what he himself had experienced, just like their witness had.

One hand lay palm up beside him, fingers slack, blood streaking the creases like he'd tried to shield himself or wipe the truth away. More blood darkened the crown of his head. He must've swiped at his face, tried to clear his vision, maybe even see his killer.

Too late.

Emma's throat tightened.

Whatever else Freddy had been, he hadn't deserved this.

A foot above their officer, blood stained the siding on the house, and Emma made out one definite indentation in it—from where the bullet had passed through their victim's body and hit the home. A .38 was in there. She knew it.

Mia nodded at Colton as he walked up and stepped aside to allow the tech walking with him to get closer to the victim.

"Meet Officer Freddy Gorik." The tech crouched next to the victim. "Thirty-three years old and a ten-year veteran of MPD."

The tech gestured to the sheet he'd pulled aside, and Emma waved for him to go ahead. She didn't have any desire to look at the man's shocked gaze longer than necessary.

Emma nodded toward the ambulance where they'd questioned Linda Weller before filling both Mia and Colton in on the specific details she, Leo, and Vance had gleaned from the witness.

"The front yard?" Mia posed the question when she was done. "Was she sure?"

"She said the FBI agent was standing under the massive oak when he fired on Freddy. Right in front of her, basically."

Mia nodded toward where Elizabeth Soyinka stood. "What about the other woman you were speaking to? She's a witness also, right?"

"Kind of, sort of." Emma sighed. "As in, she was outside during the crime, but she was focused on her child inside her minivan until the shot rang out. At that moment, she saw Linda Weller fall backward and thought she was the one who'd been shot. Elizabeth Soyinka was so focused on her neighbor, she didn't notice anything about our unsub. Maybe she'll remember something and call us, but I think she just had tunnel vision."

Colton blew out air through his nose, visibly frustrated.

Emma glanced back toward Linda Weller, attempting to sort out her own thoughts. "And both Weller and Soyinka heard a man scream to call 911. Soyinka says the voice was strong, that she didn't think it came from the victim. Weller didn't know."

"So the witness thinks our shooter told her to call 911." Colton frowned at the victim before directing his attention to the bullet hole in the siding.

"Maybe Gorik was trying to reason with the agent, confused like Darby was by what was happening." Mia's theory was valid.

Emma waved at the tech. "Can you try to dig the bullet out while we're here?" She softened her expression. "I'm sorry, I didn't get your name. But we appreciate your help."

"It's Richard." The tech moved around her and peered at the bullet hole in the house. "I can't believe we're this shorthanded. Hold on. I'll need to take photos and measurements first." He took off. To grab some tools, presumably.

"Where's the owner, by the way? Martha Lancaster?" Mia studied the road. "Wouldn't you leave your big, important job if a cop was murdered in your yard?"

Colton pulled out his phone. "I'll text Jacinda with what we've learned so far. Meanwhile, we can try to figure out why Freddy Gorik was here to begin with."

Emma nodded. Even if she remained irritated by Colton's sheer presence, having an extra brain focused on this case wasn't a bad thing right now. Brainstorming always benefited with more eyes. "Do we know if we're in the same area he normally patrolled?"

Mia nodded. "The cop I spoke to confirmed that this suburb is on the edge of Gorik's beat, so he wasn't anywhere he shouldn't have been, as far as the department's concerned."

Colton tucked his phone away. "That means it's possible he was passing through and saw something that needed to be addressed. Pulled over to do so."

Sweeping some stray hairs from her face, Emma shook her head. "If anything else was amiss, I'm pretty sure Linda

Weller would've noticed it and commented. She mentioned that the owner of this house is always at work. Seems to know her schedule and her neighbors' business in general. And she was out watering her flowers, which wouldn't have been the case if there'd been something suspicious happening before the officer and unsub showed up."

"So if nothing was happening to make Gorik pull over, he must've had a reason to come to this address and park. And that means somebody must've summoned our officer here. To a residence where no one is home." Mia pinched her chin between two fingers.

"Just like Darby had a reason to get out of his vehicle and go down that alley with his killer, who fits the same description as this one."

Mia nudged Emma, her gaze flicking toward the two figures crossing the street. She stiffened as their partners approached.

Emma caught the subtle shift in her body language and forced herself not to react. Vance was still a sore spot—for all of them. And while she appreciated Mia's protective instincts toward her, they had a ton of work to do.

As he and Leo reached their group, Emma jumped in before Mia could land the first verbal jab, filling them in on everything they knew so far.

When she asked if they'd found anything new, Leo just shook his head. Vance looked everywhere but at her.

"It's like Darby." Emma waved to the parked cruiser. "He was on his beat but got pulled into a place he normally wouldn't have had reason to go. I'd say that's what happened here if I had to guess, based on Linda Weller not seeing anything to draw law enforcement to the area beforehand."

Mia waved over the cop she'd spoken to earlier. "Did anyone call Gorik to this area prior to his attack?"

He shrugged. "You'd have to ask Dispatch to be sure, but

as far as I know, the department only learned Gorik was here when the witness called 911."

She nodded, and the cop hurried off toward the crime scene tape, where another officer was waving for backup. A second news van had arrived, and that had brought out even more curious bystanders.

Richard the tech returned with what looked like a filing tool and a wicked looking pair of tweezers. Before doing anything else, he photographed the bullet hole, holding up a measuring tape for scope. With that done, he stuck a mini flashlight between his teeth and bent close to the siding. Setting to work, he angled in the file-like tool and came out a moment later with a bullet safely between the arms of the tweezers.

Colton held up an evidence bag for the tech, and he dropped the bullet in. He shifted and held the evidence up so all five of them could view it.

Emma leaned closer to the bullet as if she were expecting it to talk to her.

She watched as Richard labeled the bag, providing chain of evidence. After he logged it, he tucked his tools away and made a gesture back at the other house as if to say, *May I?*

"Of course." Emma took the bag from Colton. "Thanks for your help." She waved him off, no longer particularly worried about being polite. "Objectively, it looks to be the same caliber as the bullet recovered at our first crime scene. A thirty-eight, slightly misshapen and squished and bloodied."

"And we know that gun was stolen from the Salem PD's armory."

Colton hit them with the biggest evidence in the case, and he'd said it so casually, like he was ordering a latte.

"Come again?" Emma was flabbergasted by the news and

did little to hide it. The bullets from a gun Celeste Foss had stolen were killing cops in D.C.

*This is bad, very bad.*

"I'm sorry. I thought you knew."

"Forensics didn't have the results in. We were just there." Leo pointed a thumb at Vance and then himself. "And then we got called here." He'd managed a calmer tone than Emma, though she could see the surprise in his eyes too.

Colton shrugged as sort of an apology. "I started doing a deep dive on Darby, found nothing, and went to ballistics. Must've just missed you guys. That's why I was late getting here."

Everyone pulled out their phones in sync and checked their email.

There it was—an update from forensics. The striations on the bullets found at Officer Greg Darby's scene were a hit with a Smith & Wesson Model 10, one of the weapons in the database of stolen arsenal from the armory in Salem.

After a string of quick glances, everyone put their phones away, realizing now was not the time to get into the Salem connection. They needed to get back to HQ to root through all this.

Emma considered their next move. *Unfortunately, until we know if this bullet is a match to the one that killed Darby, you have to stay on track, Emma girl.*

Vance looked up and down the street. "Are we sure this is part of Gorik's beat?"

*Thank you, Vance.*

Colton stuffed his hands into his pockets. "The cop confirmed it."

Leo gestured toward the chaos. "We did talk to a few people who heard the gunshot and wandered out as a result, but we got the same answer from everyone. Nothing was out of the ordinary before the gunshot. And nobody was home in a house close enough to see what might've happened. Except for our witnesses."

Emma licked her lips. "Leo, Vance, could the two of you go visit the communication center and talk to the 911 dispatchers? If we can figure out why Gorik was here to begin with, that could be worth something."

Leo said something in the affirmative just as Emma caught sight of Freddy's ghost. He wasn't close enough for her to feel the cold of the Other. She forced a smile for the benefit of her colleagues and nodded toward the fallen officer's cruiser where the ghost was wandering. "I'm going to give his vehicle a look, all right?"

Rather than waiting for an answer, she headed in the ghost's direction. The cold of the Other embraced her as she did, and she dug her hands into her windbreaker pockets to fight against it.

The ghost paced between the oak tree and his car, muttering to himself. "I never should've taken the money. Hell, that has to be it. I never should've taken the money."

Emma moved on past him toward the car, making a show of examining it, while she watched as Mia engaged an officer. Twice, the ghost paced back into earshot and kept repeating the same thing about money. And once more, there were simply too many people around for her to even think about addressing him directly.

Maybe Gorik was dirty, which would track with the attitude from Detective Fletcher. Come to think of it, none of the officers they'd spoken to had seemed particularly shaken up by Freddy Gorik's death, unlike what Emma had seen at their first crime scene, where Greg Darby was killed.

But even if Gorik had been a dirty cop, he was still a uniformed MPD officer. One of their own had fallen, and nearly the whole precinct had come out to the scene. But where did that leave them?

Sure, death could potentially have been payback from a fellow officer who was tired of his crap, but what about Darby? Was it possible the younger officer had somehow been just as dirty but better at hiding it? Or had he caught someone else acting criminally, someone like Gorik, and was killed to stay silent?

But then why kill Gorik too?

It could mean another vigilante, whether the killer was a cop or an agent...but that still didn't feel right to Emma.

Not to mention the elephant at the crime scenes—the .38 caliber bullets, one of which was already traced back to Celeste Foss.

As if to highlight the disparity, one of the cops Mia had been speaking to shot a glance toward Gorik's prone body. "Wonder if he'll stop complaining about shit now that he's dead."

The other cop beside him flinched, shooting an apologetic look to Mia. "Don't speak ill of the dead, man. He wore the uniform just like the rest of us."

Shaking his head, the other officer shrugged.

*No, these two victims weren't the same at all, Emma girl.*

Except they were both likely killed by a gun that was stolen by Celeste Foss. Which was one hell of a connection. And not just to their victims, but to Emma herself.

## 15

Leo parked near the entrance to the Washington, D.C. Office of Unified Communications. A large white-and-brown block with oversize windows, it looked much like every other office building in the capital city, if with fewer people coming and going. The place didn't exactly invite visitors, but that was the point. Just like law enforcement, dispatchers could attract plenty of anger from the public.

He gestured to Vance's phone before unbuckling his seat belt. "That latest buzz from Jacinda or someone else?"

"Jacinda, but nothing's new." Vance tucked the device away and zipped his windbreaker back up. "Said she's lighting a fire under forensics' ass to try to get some more people out to our new crime scene. They'll canvass the area for any other evidence, but it's not like the crime scene stretched for blocks. Oh, and there's a subpoena in the works for any dispatch records related to Gorik being called out, should we get any pushback here."

Stretching in his seat, Leo grimaced. "Before we get out… any new thoughts on Colton? He was frazzled when he got to the scene but seemed normal enough after that."

"I still don't trust him." Vance stared blankly through the windshield. "I mean, yeah, he was normal enough after a while, but…"

Leo drummed his fingertips across the top of the steering wheel. "Yeah. He's hiding something."

"Exactly. And, sure, Mia may think I'm paranoid to think everyone's hiding something, but in this case, I feel pretty damn justified. Maybe she's the one deflecting."

Leo forced a sympathetic expression, though the last thing he wanted to encourage was more sniping. He put his hand on the door handle. "Shall we?"

Vance opened his own door by way of reply and led the way toward the front entrance. A security pad and voice-call button greeted them. When he pressed the button, a "Can I help you?" emitted from a speaker.

Leo held his identification up toward the camera watching from above. "We're out of the FBI VCU and have some questions."

The door clicked open, and Leo pocketed his identification as they entered.

Inside, the glow of blue screen light offset recessed lighting from above. Short-walled cubicles ranged out ahead of them, with serious-faced men and women in headsets at every one.

No matter how many times Leo entered one of these places, the low, urgent voices of 911 dispatchers never failed to awe him. Organized chaos had never been a more fitting term than for what transpired between callers, dispatchers, and the first responders who were called in turn, but these places still somehow radiated an impression of calm.

Equivalent to the calm before the storm, he supposed. Still. Give him a siren and a gun any day, and he'd be more comfortable than sitting on a headset and trying to organize rescues from afar.

A young woman looked up from her desk, squinting at the two of them as if they were a foreign species. "Are you looking for someone specific?"

Leo flashed his badge just as Vance did, though he guessed this was the same woman who'd spoken up before allowing them entrance. "We're looking for whoever's in charge. Please."

The woman let out a low hum. "You want Charlie, then. Keep to the left wall, and you'll find his office in the back left corner, near the stairwell. I'll let him know you're coming."

Skirting the wide area of cubicles and dispatchers, Leo moved as directed. The entire left wall was covered with the smiling faces of valued employees who'd been honored or retired from the communications center, and by the time they reached Charlie's door, Leo felt as if he'd been down a whole hall of examining eyes.

The way every dispatcher looked at him and Vance suspiciously as they moved, even if they didn't say anything, didn't help.

A large man with glasses and a dark-brown goatee opened the door just as Leo raised his hand to knock. He looked back and forth between the two of them, wiped sweaty bangs from his eyes, then held out his hand to shake each of theirs. "Charlie Dunn, 911 dispatch manager. How can I help you?"

He gave a cursory nod to their IDs but focused more on their faces. Trusting his front desk for the gatekeeping, Leo guessed.

"Special Agents Leo Ambrose and Vance Jessup. Could we talk in your office?"

The man backed up and waved them in. As soon as the door shut behind them, Leo began explaining the situation. When he'd finished, Charlie was back behind his desk.

Vance gestured at the computer. "Is there any way you

can verify whether or not someone was called to a specific location?"

"Sure." Charlie turned to his keyboard. "Hell, you could've called if that's all you needed. Take a card for next time."

Leo did as instructed, grabbing a card from the holder on the edge of the man's desk. Vance did the same after a moment.

Soon, though, Charlie was shaking his head.

"This afternoon, the nearest call to that area was a house fire about a mile off. Firefighters were dispatched, but it was just a kitchen fire. No police response was required. Doesn't look like your officer's car was dispatched to anything after…eleven this morning. I can go through all the calls that came in around the time of his murder if you want me to. If a call for police aid isn't recorded in the system already, it didn't happen."

Leo fought back a sigh. "No, that won't be necessary. Can you tell us what that eleven o'clock call was?"

"Sure." Charlie typed at his computer some more. "Gorik responded to a traffic accident over near the Preston Shopping Center, about five miles away from your crime scene. Busy area like that, wouldn't surprise me to hear the scene tied him up for hours."

Making a mental note to check that out with the precinct, Leo jotted down the location.

"Thanks for your time, Charlie." He stood and tucked the man's card away. "We'll call if we need anything else. Maybe just give a listen to the calls made in the hour or so before Gorik was shot, if it's not too much trouble?"

"Sure thing. Nothing's too much trouble for a fallen first responder."

Vance nodded a thanks.

Charlie settled deeper into his chair. "I'll do it now and be able to tell you if I find anything by day's end."

With an additional nod of thanks, Leo led the way back out of the office and toward the SUV. They needed to call Emma and Jacinda to fill them in.

Whatever that officer had been doing at their crime scene, he hadn't been summoned there on official business.

## 16

Emma hung up with Leo just as she and Mia stepped into the Eighth Precinct. The hall still smelled faintly of bleach and tired coffee, and every officer they passed looked like they hadn't slept in a week.

It hadn't taken long for the medical examiner's van to collect Officer Freddy Gorik's body, and the forensic team had already cleared the suburban property where he'd been shot. MPD would handle the scene reconstruction and evidence cataloging, but Emma had asked to personally deliver the initial report—and one sealed evidence bag—to Chief Ebenstein.

She carried it now, tucked under one arm. It contained Gorik's personal items, bagged and logged by the city techs. His phone. His wallet. A few other everyday carry pieces. And so much cash.

*"I never should've taken that money."*

Was that why he was killed? Not as a robbery, but as a lesson?

The gun stayed with ballistics for comparison to the Darby shooting.

Beside her, Mia checked her phone, brow furrowed. "Leo didn't get anything from Dispatch?"

Emma shook her head. "No record of Gorik being called to that address. Whoever lured him there didn't go through any official channels."

Mia popped a mint into her mouth, offering one to Emma, who took it gratefully.

"Somebody might've summoned Gorik there, but it wasn't Dispatch or for any official police business. Leo said he texted Jacinda the update, but I'm thinking we call in and see if she can get us access to Gorik's personal cell."

They ducked into an empty office, and Mia placed the call.

"Anything new to report?" Jacinda sounded stressed and irritated through the speaker.

"We're at the precinct now." Mia leaned against the wall. "The M.E. took Gorik, and forensics took his car, though, at a glance, there wasn't anything inside his cruiser that screamed 'new evidence.' You got Leo's update?"

"I did. What are you thinking?"

Emma didn't want to tell her how she was reeling from the Celeste Foss connection to Darby's crime or her suspicions that Gorik's bullet would be from the same gun—that would be an in-person conversation.

She leaned toward the phone, speaking up. "We still think Gorik must've been summoned there by someone. The techs collected his personal cell phone from the body. It's a phone wallet with a ton of cash inside. Any chance you could get us rushed access to his financials and phone?"

"I'll make some calls." Jacinda paused, the faintest sound of computer keys tapping in the background. "I'm also still trying to see if we can somehow link the officer to Martha Lancaster, the owner of the house, just in case she had reason to make a personal call. The owner hasn't shown up yet, I take it?"

"Not by the time we left." Mia rolled her shoulders, the joints popping several times. "You said she's some kind of techie?"

"Yes, and one who doesn't answer her phone." Jacinda grunted. "But either way, linking her to Gorik is looking less and less likely, the more digging I do. She's a computer geek, works for some AI company. Clean as a whistle, even if she doesn't answer her phone."

"Sounds like something MPD will want to handle. Even if Gorik didn't have the greatest reputation, he was still one of their own." Emma frowned at the memory of where the officer had taken his last breaths. "Do you want us to head back to HQ to discuss the findings on the first bull—"

"No, I know it's on your mind, Emma. Mine, too, but have another chat with Chief Ebenstein first. About Gorik this time. Then we'll all meet back here for a late dinner, compare notes, and talk about that stolen gun."

Emma's lips tightened as Mia signed off the call. If she could get the team together, minus Colton, it was time to tell everyone about Darby's ghost talking about how the "night" should've been "all right," and Gorik's ghost saying he "shouldn't have taken the money." They had to be clues. Even if Vance ended up flipping out over another supernatural occurrence, she couldn't wait any longer.

*Not when our killer is very likely targeting another cop at this very moment.*

Emma wasn't surprised to find Chief Brooks Ebenstein waiting for them when they reached the precinct. She'd called ahead to let him know they were coming, hoping he'd still be around even at half past six in the evening. As promised, the man was leaning against the wall across from the elevators when the doors opened. He'd been cleaning his glasses and replaced them above his nose to reach out and shake their hands.

"Agent Last, Agent Logan. I can't say it's good to see you. Getting a little tired of it, if you don't mind me saying."

Emma offered a sympathetic nod. "I understand, Chief. We're sorry for your losses."

His face scrunched up just a touch, then he turned with a wave, gesturing for them to follow. "Come on into the office. You might as well. With two of my people down, we need this bastard found ASAP."

Once Emma and Mia had seated themselves across from him, he tented his hands over his belly and leaned back in his chair.

"Chief," Mia pulled her tablet out, resting it on her knees, "if you could tell us about Officer Freddy Gorik, we'd appreciate it."

He ran his tongue out over his lips as he seemed to consider the question. "I want to tell you first that he never worked with Greg Darby. I can't see how the two of them are connected, no matter how I look at things. Gorik was on the force for about ten years compared to Darby's one, and he always worked a daytime beat. Got called in to back up our detectives normally because he was so well-known around here, but Darby was just a nighttime beat cop. Totally different circles."

"So you're thinking the killer targeted them randomly?" That didn't sound good to Emma. With no connection, it meant there were potentially two cop killers dressed like FBI agents out there.

"I don't know how your investigation is going, and I'm not trying to butt in, understand, but our guys are busting their asses on legwork to try to get this guy found. Knocking on doors, searching through Darby's and Gorik's cases, you name it. Everything points to it being random. Except for the presence of the FBI." The chief shifted in his chair, meeting her eyes.

Emma could feel the man putting up walls, brick by brick, with each word he said.

"Since I can't afford to keep losing good cops, you'll have to excuse me for speaking my mind. We need to find this bastard before he attacks another cop. And I need to know you're digging into your own people too."

Emma gave a grim nod. "No excusing necessary. And I think we're making progress in the investigation, but it's not going as fast as we'd like. We're certainly keeping every avenue open. If you could tell us about Officer Gorik, that'd be very helpful."

"Right, right." The chief typed at his keyboard for a moment, then faced her again. "Gorik was a good cop. He got a commendation from the mayor a few years back, for being at the forefront of busting a big drug ring. The man knew how to complain, I admit, and that got on some people's nerves, but there are worse vices."

Mia's eyes narrowed. "You're saying he made enemies on the force?"

"Not *enemies*." The chief removed his glasses and rubbed his eyes. "He just wasn't as buddy-buddy with the rest of the precinct as a lot of my other officers. But he got shit done, and he did it the right way. Like I said, he was a good cop."

Emma waited for the chief to continue, but he'd gone silent. Before she could prod him, his phone buzzed.

Looking down at it, he nodded as if to himself. "You've got Gorik's personal cell phone on you? I just got the code needed to unlock it."

Emma pulled out the bagged phone and placed it on the desk, keeping it carefully sealed. The device had already been dusted, but it hadn't been swabbed for DNA. She'd promised forensics she'd drop it off after their conversation with the chief, hoping for this very outcome.

Carefully, trying not to put a hole in the bag, she opened the phone wallet. She was reminded of the big surprise they had for the good chief.

"Chief, I hate to ask, but do you have any idea why Gorik would've been carrying this much cash?" She gave the stack another look. "The tech who catalogued his personal items counted a thousand dollars in twenties here."

Ebenstein's eyes narrowed. "That all came out of Gorik's wallet?"

Emma shook her head. "His phone case, which can serve as a wallet, as you can see. But his regular wallet had thirty-some dollars in it." She showed him the opened compartment of Gorik's phone wallet through the baggy.

He sat back in his chair with a huff. "Shit. I don't know. But a cop carrying that much cash when we're between paydays…and while on shift? That makes me nervous."

Emma set the bagged phone back beside her tablet in her bag.

"Gorik was complaining about bills last week." The chief stretched, looking past Emma to the bullpen behind them without really focusing on it. "Talking about how cops should earn more. Sounded like the same old bellyaching to me. I asked if I should know about anything else, any trouble he was dealing with, and he said no. I told him to talk to his union rep."

The chief let out a dark, angry chuckle, and Emma finally held up the phone again. "Chief, I'm sorry to ask, but it's more important than ever that we get into this phone."

He glanced back to her as if surprised, then nodded and picked up his own phone. "Right. Code his wife sent me is four-two-six-two-one-one."

Through the plastic, Emma pressed the button on the side of the device. The main screen came up in seconds. Gorik's wallpaper was a picture of a police shield, and he didn't have many apps. Emma pulled up his call history, and her pulse immediately sped up at what she saw.

Mia must've sensed her surprise, as she leaned in. "Last call was an unknown number."

"It lines up time-wise...came in about twenty minutes before he was shot." Emma checked the length of the call. "Just over a minute long."

Ebenstein leaned forward. "Your team's thinking he was lured to the scene where he was shot? Maybe the money was involved somehow?"

Emma pursed her lips, but she nodded hesitantly. "It's possible."

She shared a glance with Mia, though, and could tell from her narrowed eyes that they were both thinking the same thing. If the money were involved, and Gorik took the money for some nefarious purpose, why did he still have it? Wouldn't the money have been exchanged?

Either way, they needed to get back to HQ and share what they'd learned.

Emma went to the device settings and unlocked the phone before setting it back down. She looked back at Ebenstein. "Could you provide information on every case Gorik was working recently? Say, going back a few months?"

He scribbled a note to himself. "I'll get you the information on the last six months of cases if it'll help, no problem. Anything to find this guy. You just let me know if you need anything else."

Emma stood up and shook his hand as Mia stowed her tablet and offered her sympathies once more. The chief might not be wrong about Gorik having been a good cop, but if he was a clean cop—that was another question. And in any case, Ebenstein's grief was real, as was his justified frustration.

They needed to find this killer before he managed to steal any more police officers away from this precinct or any other.

## 17

Emma finished wrapping up what they'd discovered about Gorik—including his stash of twenties—and then gazed around the conference table at her colleagues, including Colton Wright. Even their latest addition seemed taken aback by the new evidence.

The whiteboard was littered with a string of unconnected facts. And a very big connection—the murder weapon in the first killing was connected to Salem, which meant Darby's murder might be connected to their previous cases.

Leo sat back in his chair, drumming his fingers on the table. "It can't be a coincidence that he got that call from an unknown number and had all that money on him at the crime scene."

Jacinda nodded. "And I had MPD check the tracking on his vehicle after Emma called. As soon as that call came in, he headed to a gas station and then beelined for that address where he was killed."

"Gas stations have ATMs..." Emma ran her palm across the smooth conference table, the touch of its cool surface grounding her thoughts. "Are we thinking he was being blackmailed?"

Jacinda offered a tight smile. "It's possible. We're working on getting the security footage from the gas station he stopped at. Maybe we can confirm he took the money out while we wait for warrants on his financials."

Vance sat forward. "But if we can figure out who killed him by tracing the phone number, that may lead us directly to the unsub."

"Or," Colton shook his head, "we could be on totally the wrong track, and he received that money from someone. Or was simply getting it out because someone needed it. That call could've come from someone needing financial help."

"There are a lot of possibilities, obviously." Emma chose her words carefully. What she really wanted was to tell the rest of her team about Gorik's ghost and what he'd said about taking money, but she couldn't do that with Colton sitting here. "But if he was going to deliver it, who was he giving it to? Our unsub?"

Colton nodded, meeting her gaze as if they were on the same page. "And if he'd just received it, when did he have time to stuff it in his wallet before getting himself killed?"

Mia shook her head. "It wasn't in his *wallet* wallet. It was in his phone-case wallet. I still think he must've picked it up during that stop. Why would our unsub hand over a thousand dollars and not retrieve it after killing him? Or if our unsub was after the money, why didn't he take it before killing Gorik? They'd had an exchange, according to Linda Weller. It doesn't make sense."

Colton fidgeted in his seat, and Emma took an extra second to examine him. When they'd still been waiting for Jacinda to come in, he'd seemed uncomfortable. Conflicted at best and racked with nerves at worst. His tie was loosened, and his hair was greasy, as if he'd spent an hour or two running his hands through it. When he caught her gaze, he flushed.

*Act friendly, Emma girl.*

But though she'd meant for her small smile to lower his walls, it did the opposite. While Leo was mid-sentence, talking about how small a bribe a thousand dollars would be —if that'd been what it was—Colton shot to his feet.

"I need you all to excuse me for a moment. Please." Without another word, he backed away from the table, nearly knocking his chair into the wall, and hightailed it out the door.

Emma didn't waste any time. In seconds, she jumped to her feet and moved to make sure the door was solidly closed. Standing beside it, leaning against the wall, she faced the group. "Sorry to interrupt, Leo, but this can't wait. I saw Gorik's ghost at the scene. He was muttering about how he shouldn't have taken the money."

Vance threw his hands up. "You've got to be kidding me. And you're telling us now?"

"It's the first chance she's had!" Mia glared at him.

Emma ignored them both. "And I saw Darby's ghost, who kept muttering…hold on." She closed her eyes. "He said, 'Still looking for night. Night was supposed to be all right…' Darby's message is cryptic, per usual."

Mia considered it. "It was still dark out at five in the morning. Night, if you will. Doesn't tell us much, though."

Leo raised an eyebrow.

Vance turned to face Jacinda. "These messages don't prove anything. It's clear something's up with the money Gorik had on him."

Jacinda looked skeptical. "But at the very least, her seeing Gorik and hearing what she did tells us he took that money…"

"Or *some* money he shouldn't have. Vance is right that it doesn't prove much." Emma's admission deepened Jacinda's scowl. "But it does seem to suggest he was less than the great cop Ebenstein thought he was."

"It proves the money was directly related to his murder, or at least Gorik's ghost thinks it is."

Emma appreciated Leo's support. "Yes."

"Wait a sec." Vance sat up straighter. "It's not *night* as in *nighttime*. It's *knight* as in shining armor, or someone's last name. Knight with a *K*. Isn't that what Linda Weller said she thought she heard, the cop called him Knight or Nile?"

Jacinda slapped the table, excitement brightening her features. "Which would almost definitively mean we're looking for the same unsub. If Darby's ghost thought 'Knight was all right,' and the witness at Gorik's crime scene heard the agent use the same name…same description, same FBI uniform. Same killer, most likely."

Leo pushed himself up from the table and paced along the other side of it before finally leaning against the wall across from Emma. "So we have an unsub to catch who goes by Knight. We can check the database, but chances of it being a real name are slim. I think we still have to consider Colton, that the unsub is an actual FBI agent. Did you see how uncomfortable he was, Jacinda? Earlier? And then the way he left so suddenly?"

Jacinda closed her eyes and sat back in her seat, taking a deep breath before focusing on them again. "We've been over this, Leo…"

"I agree with him." Vance sat forward, his gaze drilling into Jacinda. "And, hell, if Emma's focused on the Other, and the bullets are from a stolen gun from Salem, that doesn't mean Colton's not involved. He could be a witch."

Emma fought the urge to roll her eyes. "Nothing suggests that, Vance."

"He fits the profile."

"You fit the profile." Emma inhaled deeply, striving for calm. "I'd say the gun from Salem eliminates Colton as a suspect, if anything."

"As would I." Jacinda's raised voice silenced the debate, though Vance sat back with a huff. "And what Emma heard supports the idea that Gorik was being blackmailed or was involved in something outside the bounds of his normal police duties."

Leo's gaze found Emma's, almost apologetic as he shook his head. "Not everything has a supernatural explanation. And surely we have plenty of avenues to take. Let's look into all Knights in the system, retired, deceased, active, for starters. Let's follow the money with Gorik."

"Call the number that contacted Gorik, find the phone tower, narrow down the location." Mia ticked off their most urgent actions on their to-do list on her fingers.

Emma pulled out a sticky note with the number on it and handed it to her, then she glanced out the interior window, but Colton was still nowhere to be found. As oddly as the man acted, though, she didn't suspect him. "I think our best line of pursuit is looking into any recent cases where Gorik might've gotten wrapped up in something illegal. If we want to get somewhere off the evidence we have, that's what we should do."

Vance opened his mouth to argue, but Jacinda put a hand up. "I agree with Emma."

Still seated at the table, Mia nodded, and although Leo's frown suggested doubt, he didn't argue.

Jacinda turned to Emma. "Examine the cases Gorik was on. That's our next step. But…" She glanced around the table, deflated. "None of us has had dinner, and it's coming up on seven thirty. That's my fault because I meant to order food and forgot. Let's call it a night and reconvene first thing tomorrow. We'll look into Gorik then. Go home and get some sleep."

Emma looked at the whiteboard.

Barnaby was being paid to kill and drop the bodies where law enforcement would find them.

He had a female accomplice—or *he* was the accomplice—in the kidnapping of Vance. She was still at-large.

He had a photo of Emma from Quantico in his apartment.

He wrote the handwritten note found on one murder victim, but the two emails were likely not from him.

Officer Greg Darby was a young, by-the-books cop murdered on federal property with a Smith & Wesson Model 10, one Celeste Foss stole from the Salem PD armory.

Officer Freddy Gorik was a not-so-clean cop murdered with what appeared to be a .38 caliber bullet too. He was carrying a thousand dollars in cash and got called to a suburban neighborhood, midday, where he was killed in front of a witness, who might've heard the shooter yell at her to call 911.

An old dark-green Toyota RAV4 was seen leaving Gorik's crime scene.

Darby's ghost and Gorik's witness, Linda Weller, confirmed that "Knight" was the name of their killer. And Gorik's ghost told her that "taking the money" was likely what got him killed. Neither of those facts were on the board, of course.

Emma knew in her heart that the second bullet would link to the gun from Salem.

*Are they sending you a message, Emma girl? And is* they *a she? The very person Celeste Foss warned you against?*

Emma turned and opened the door before the team could keep arguing about Colton, though she had no intention of calling it a night.

*Sure, I could sleep and wake up to bad news.*

*Or I could order in and finish this before I have to go back to Ebenstein's office to talk about another dead cop.*

No matter what her team might have planned, she knew her choice.

## 18

Leo followed Vance to his desk, though he searched the area for Colton as he moved. The mystery agent was still gone. He leaned in toward Vance to speak, keeping his voice low. "You thinking what I'm thinking?"

Vance gazed around the area, scratching at his butterfly bandage, before giving a short nod. "Where'd our guy go?"

Bingo. "I think we should find out."

Mia and Emma had disappeared into the breakroom, but Leo led the way out toward the elevators. He ducked into the men's room first, but it was empty.

When he came back to the front of the elevators, Vance shook his head. "No sign of him down the hall or in the copy room. Our guy disappeared. Want to check the garage?"

Leo zeroed in on the light coat still slung across his chair. "His stuff's here. I say we just wait. He's bound to show up."

Vance didn't look convinced but nodded. "Jacinda may insist he's innocent, but she didn't say we can't ask about his behavior. It's past time to get some answers."

Leo was about to ask if it should be a team effort, but the elevator door opened to reveal Colton tucking his phone back into his pocket. He froze, but only for a moment before stepping out. "Meeting over, I take it?"

Vance shook his head and walked off, but Leo stepped closer to Colton. His tie was loose. His hair was mussed. He had bags under his eyes. The man was stressed about something.

"Who've you been disappearing to chat with on the phone? If you're supposed to be helping us, you're spending an awful lot of time talking to someone who's not on this team."

Colton's eyes widened, and he stepped back, hitting the wall. His gaze went to Vance before coming back to Leo's.

*Am I imagining this guy's breaking out in a cold sweat right before my very eyes?*

"It's nothing you need to concern yourselves with. Don't we have a killer to find?"

Vance came back over, so that the three of them were a tight triangle by the wall. He slowly peeled off the bandage on his forehead. Leo found the move surprisingly intimidating. "Where were you when Gorik was killed? Where do you keep going?"

Leo watched the man's brow wrinkle and his lips tighten. Colton was breathing heavier now, nerves getting the better of him.

"I was looking into Darby and then the bullet, like I said." He crossed his arms over his chest, then seemed to think better of the defensive posture and offered a fake-sounding laugh that didn't reach his eyes. "What are the two of you accusing me of?"

Leo shrugged, knowing the gesture came off as being just as fake as Colton's laugh. "We're working together, Agent Wright. Seems like we should know a little bit more about you."

He stood straighter, glaring. "You two jackasses really

think I'm your killer? Is that it? I'm here to fucking support you. To help with the case. Scrutinizing every little action I take won't accomplish anything."

"Even if you're acting suspicious?" Vance's jibe stilled the other agent, and for a second, Leo thought he might throw a punch, but instead, he suddenly deflated.

"Just leave me alone so I can do my job. Can you do that? I'll do mine, and you'll do yours, and maybe with any luck, we'll catch our cop killer. If that's okay with you." Colton pushed off the wall and strode between them, heading back toward his too-clean desk.

Leo stared after him, torn between his own suspicions and Jacinda's clear dismissal of them. Was he focusing in on Colton Wright just because he was the only possibility for a suspect right now, however remote?

He didn't know anymore. But the man was hiding something, and whatever it was, Leo suspected that something had to do with this case or the team.

Which option would be easier to deal with, he wasn't entirely sure.

# 19

Emma plucked some fried rice from her legal pad and put it on top of the napkin with the other bits of Chinese food she'd dropped while reading. She never had perfected the art of eating rice with chopsticks and didn't know why she'd thought to try tonight. Particularly when she was barely looking at her food, no matter how sweet it smelled. Not when she had Freddy Gorik's case files laid out in front of her on her monitor.

They'd hardly left for the night, but at least they were sticking together, as Jacinda had suggested after finding Emma's photo at Barnaby's. Now, with the bullets belonging to a gun from Salem that Celeste had stolen, it seemed more important than ever.

Mia had called the phone number to no avail. It pinged off a few towers but then got lost by the river walk. The unsub might've tossed it.

Leo grunted at something on his own computer but remained focused on files when she looked up. He'd been in a bit of a huff ever since the earlier meeting when they'd put off his suspicions about Colton, so she let him be and went back to her research.

For the most part, the results all looked pretty standard. Emma had been searching for any indication Gorik might've gotten paid to keep his mouth shut but had, so far, turned up nothing. Beside her, Leo made a note on his trusty legal pad while stuffing half of an eggroll into his mouth.

*He won the food choice battle tonight. Grease be damned.*

"Find anything interesting?"

He pointed to his cheek in the age-old signal for chewing, continuing to study his legal pad. When he looked up, though, he only frowned. "I've been looking into that big drug case he closed. The one he got the commendation for? But the thing is, even though it was high profile, there were so many moving pieces and lawyers involved, I don't see how any of the cops could've been shady."

Emma nodded to the legal pad. "What did you write down, then?"

"That we were dealing with some missing evidence." He glanced doubtfully at the notation. "I can look into it, but they didn't ultimately need it. Doesn't seem like he could've been bribed to steal extraneous evidence when he had so much on the line."

Looking back at the monitor with a sigh, Emma shook her head. "Especially not when he had so much to lose, it being a high profile case."

"Listen…" Leo nudged his chair closer to her desk, and she picked up the remains of her meal and focused on him. "Vance and I talked to Colton before he left. He was up in arms about us asking questions."

"Leo, come on…" Emma sat back in her seat, plopping her food carton back onto her desk. "Haven't you heard a word Jacinda's said?"

"He's hiding something…"

"So are we!" Emma glared at him, and he had the grace to look abashed, but it still didn't stop him.

"He shows up after Darby's murder."

"Bad timing on the Bureau's part, not his."

"He was late to Gorik's murder—"

"That's your evidence? Would you rather he be a killer than surveilling our team, seriously?"

His lip quirked. "You reading my mind now?"

She turned back to her desk with a snort. "Unbelievable. Just focus on the files if you want to help me, okay? Please?"

"Yes, ma'am."

Emma closed out a file related to expensive shoplifting. The arrestee got probation and was a first-time offender, and on top of that, he'd been stealing a gift for his mom. Not exactly the type that would end up bribing a cop for any reason.

*The next report, though...*

"Leo, look at this." She pointed to the report, skimming it for the details. "Look how vague this is."

His eyebrows knitted together. "Looks like an average report."

"Not compared to Gorik's others." She pulled up some of the ones she'd minimized, comparing the amount their dead officer had written. "See this? Even the reports on shoplifting and DUIs are more detailed. Dollars to doughnuts, Gorik's talent for writing detailed reports is one of the reasons Ebenstein praised him so much, but then we get to this one..."

"I see it, I see it." Leo leaned forward, pressing his chair closer as he read over her shoulder. "So somebody saw some guns getting moved and called the police, and Gorik was assigned to go check things out...hell, there's barely any detail here. What the hell did he see? What even was he searching for?"

Emma scrolled down the report. "He made one arrest, of someone named Rick Dwyer."

Leo rolled back to his computer and typed the name in as Emma reread the sparse report to see if she'd missed anything. "The case never went to trial. Just disappeared, and our Rick Dwyer was released from custo…holy shit."

"What?" Emma twisted to see what Leo had found. He was staring open-mouthed at his computer.

She moved sideways to see the mug shot for Rick Dwyer. It was a dead ringer for Agent Colton Wright. "Holy shit is right."

Leo tapped a pen against the screen, practically bouncing in his seat. "Vance and I were right. He must've been involved in the weapons exchange that Gorik was called to investigate. Colton got arrested, or Dwyer or whatever his real name is, and whoever Colton was working for paid off Gorik to make the case disappear. Colton would know that, and he must've blackmailed Gorik over it."

*Or you're going off the deep end, Leo, buddy.*

Emma sat back in her seat and crossed her arms. She didn't need to say anything. Just stared at her partner to get her point across.

He frowned at her. "What? It makes sense!"

"An agent blackmails a cop, risking his entire reputation, then kills the cop after going to all the trouble of blackmailing him? Leo…"

"Gorik knew who he was!" Leo leaned forward, elbows on his knees as he spoke fast. "Think about it. If Gorik recognized Colton and reported him as an agent working for some weapons dealer, he'd lose everything. Colton probably figured he'd get ahead of any trouble by killing him. Maybe he blackmailed him just to get him to a specific location. Didn't even care about the money because it was just a ruse, and…"

The excitement in Leo's voice fed on adrenaline and an *I told you so* moment. He was letting his idea run away with him, despite logic.

Sighing, Emma met his eyes and evened her voice. "Are you listening to yourself? Do you really have it in for this guy that badly? Think about what you're saying. 'Colton figured he'd get ahead of any trouble by…killing him?' The mug shot is weird, I agree, but if Colton's really just a low-level criminal, how did he get in with the FBI?"

"Maybe he's impersonating an agent." But Leo frowned, and Emma saw the truth. He was starting to have doubts in his own supposition. Still, he kept going. "A clever hacker could've set up the situation with his files going missing. A damn twin or doppelgänger."

Emma shook her head, almost amused at the theories he was tossing out. "Didn't Jacinda say the file was being withheld, not missing?"

"Jacinda just said they refused her request." Leo sat back in his seat, tapping his pen against his desk and leaving small blue marks along the surface. He'd be scrubbing them off tomorrow, she knew. "Maybe now he's here to keep tabs on the investigation of Gorik's murder. Make sure it doesn't get solved. Darby could've been a distraction, something to make us think we're looking for a serial killer instead of someone focused on Gorik. All that would explain why he's acting so strangely."

"I don't buy it. You're suggesting a crap ton of premeditation, considering Colton was assigned to us before either cop was killed." Emma pointed to the mug shot, in which the agent's hair was longer than they knew it to be. A dark bruise cut across one cheek, and a tattoo she assumed was fake decorated his neck. "Doesn't it seem a lot more likely that Colton was undercover and got arrested? The case would've been thrown out when they discovered he was an *undercover agent*."

Though Emma could see she'd gotten through to him, Leo sat back at his desk, still tapping the pen in thought. "Okay, but that doesn't mean he's innocent. He's up to something. It's possible he's a dirty agent who wormed his way into the position of spying on our team. And either way, isn't it suspicious that he got on our team and is linked to a case involving one of our victims?"

Opening her mouth to argue, Emma froze before she could. She didn't like a coincidence any more than Leo did, and this was a big one. "Okay. You're right about that much. Let's take it to Jacinda and see what she says."

They both stood.

"And if she laughs us out of her office, you owe me dinner after we finish up this case, and you owe Colton an apology for being such a jackass about him."

Leo snorted. "Funny, that's what he called us earlier."

## 20

Emma knocked on Jacinda's office door, hating to interrupt her SSA when she looked so deep in thought. Jacinda jolted before squinting at them through the window.

"Come on in!" She rubbed her bloodshot eyes as they entered. She looked exhausted. Beside her, the Chinese they'd ordered for her sat barely touched. "What are you still doing here? I thought the revised plan was you were going to eat and then go get some rest."

"We were going through Gorik's case files." Leo hefted his tablet. "Mind if we show you something?"

Jacinda reluctantly nodded, and Emma watched her brace herself for the news incoming.

Leo set the tablet down facing her, displaying Colton Wright's mug shot, and Emma watched as Jacinda's eyes widened. Before she could say a word, Leo went into a long explanation of his theory, which Emma followed with her own.

She ended with, "And remember what Officer Greg Darby's ghost said. 'Still looking for night. Night was supposed to be all right…'"

Jacinda waved a hand. "And?"

"We assumed *night* was the name *Knight*, but what if *right*...as in *all right*...wasn't just a word? What if it was a name too? *Wright*?"

Jacinda let out a soft groan and rolled her eyes. "Don't you think that's reaching?"

Emma shrugged. "Isn't that what you pay us to do? Examine every crack, chase down every maybe, toss out every wild theory until one finally sticks?"

Jacinda didn't respond right away. Her gaze dropped to the mug shot again, lips pressing into a thin line.

Leo leaned in. "We're not saying it's a lock. We're saying it's close enough to warrant a second look."

"Honestly, all of this feels far-fetched." Jacinda sighed and scrubbed her face with both hands. "If you didn't have his mug shot attached to the case, and I didn't recognize him myself, I'd say you were both nuts. But you're not."

Leo looked exasperated. "Jacinda—"

Jacinda held up a hand. "I know you don't trust him, Leo. But you've got no real motive for him killing Gorik, or at least none that stands up to the sniff test, and you're forgetting that I got orders to include Colton in the investigation before any of this happened. They came directly from upstairs. I'm guessing Emma's right that he was undercover, and the fact that he interacted with our victim is, much as I hate to say it, just a coincidence."

Leo's expression went flat with disappointment.

"Jacinda, Colton does seem to be up to something."

Jacinda raised an eyebrow and tucked some long red strands of hair behind her ear. "Are you going back on what you said about this being from an undercover op?"

"No! That's not what I mean." Emma sighed. "I just... something's up with him. I agree with Leo on that much. He's jumpy."

Leo dropped into a chair. "If he's got experience as an undercover agent, why's he doing such a bad job of blending in and acting like one of the team? I watched him literally break out in a sweat earlier."

Jacinda didn't say anything for a few moments. Finally, she shut Leo's tablet cover and handed it back. "Everyone just needs to go home and get some sleep. I'll look into the situation with Colton, but I'll be the one doing it. You understand? I will do it."

"First thing tomorrow?" Leo leaned forward, holding her gaze.

"First thing tomorrow, I promise. I'll march upstairs like Joan of Arc and demand some answers."

Emma knew that wasn't true, but Leo pushed himself to his feet and mumbled a "good night" before leaving, nonetheless. She made a more dignified exit but didn't feel any better about the way the meeting had gone.

Thing was, she wasn't even sure what end result she wanted.

When she caught up to Leo at his desk, she waited until he met her eyes. "Jacinda told us to get out of here, but she didn't specifically say *we* can't talk to Colton."

Pausing as he was pulling on his jacket, Leo glanced at the SSA's office. A small smile played on his lips. "When? We don't know where he lives. I don't even have his number."

Emma shrugged. "I'm not saying we go comb the streets for him now, but we can meet tomorrow morning at seven and make sure we catch him before he comes upstairs."

Leo's smile dimmed a little, as if he'd expected Emma *would* want to go comb the streets or find a way to show up on his doorstep, but then he gave a little nod. "Let's do it."

As much as Leo's attitude amused her, though, Emma couldn't help thinking that it proved just how much he distrusted their new team member. Getting into the elevator beside Leo, she remained silent, considering it. No way would she be sleeping well tonight, but she had to try. They all needed it, and working themselves to exhaustion wouldn't move the case forward.

When the elevator dinged, she shot out.

Half a step behind her, Leo caught Emma's arm and pulled her back into the alcove that housed the elevators. "Did you see that?"

She glanced around. "See what? Cars? The garage?"

He grumbled something she couldn't quite make out under his breath. "Colton just climbed into a sedan. A blue one. Peek out and look to your left."

Half thinking her partner was imagining things, she nevertheless peered around the corner. Sure enough, she caught the other agent's profile in a car just pulling out of a spot.

*What the hell is he still doing here?*

Emma watched the shiny sedan, an Acura TLX that looked brand-spanking-new, idle while another car backed out of a spot, then continue on down the lane at a sedate pace.

Leo nudged her elbow, smiling tightly. "Let's tail him. See where he goes. If we get the chance to question him, we do it."

"Jacinda'll kill us." Despite that, Emma gave Leo a wink. "But if you're in, I'm in."

Lunging ahead of her, Leo made a beeline for his pickup "I'm driving."

"Like hell you are." Emma redirected him to her Prius.

## 21

Emma's forte, despite popular belief, was not speeding. She was a master when it came to tailing suspects. From street to street, in the city and then on the turnpike, she stayed a perfect distance back from Colton's car.

"Helps that it's that bright, shiny blue." Leo was muttering. "Where do you think he's going?"

Emma peered at another exit sign flying by. "Home? To dinner? On a date? Who the hell knows. But if you're asking if I think he's going after another cop…"

"You don't." Leo spoke flatly, a sigh on the end of it. "Honestly, I guess maybe I don't either. But he's too suspicious for us to keep ignoring, and I don't think my theory's impossible."

Rather than argue, Emma changed lanes and the subject. "While we're waiting for him to get to where he's going, what have you been thinking of Mia and Vance's passive-aggressive shit show?"

Leo barked a surprised laugh. Emma didn't feel guilty for calling out Mia and Vance. It wasn't as if she could talk about their behavior with anyone else, and there was no question in her mind that he'd noticed.

"I'm just waiting for it to be over." He stretched his fingers around the grab handle, leaning back and allowing some of the tension out of his body. "I thought they'd have made up by now, but them breaking up would be better at this point, as long as it means we don't have to go through the sniping again."

Emma shifted sideways, just far enough to glimpse Colton's vehicle in clear sight. "Yeah, I know what you mean. The truth is, though, I can't stop feeling guilty about it. I started it, after all. I just don't know if it's my place to step in and try to…hell, I don't know. Fix it? Bring it to a head? Tell them to get over themselves? Or…"

Leo shook his head and patted Emma's shoulder in a fashion that felt more grandfatherly than anything he'd ever done, including his Sunday-afternoon driving style. "It's not your fault, Emma. Your unique skill set has absolutely nothing to do with their relationship."

"But…"

"But nothing."

Emma glimpsed the other agent's car three vehicles ahead, moving into an exit lane. "If they had it in them to act like this to each other over my confession, something was bound to trigger it eventually between the two of them. Maybe it's just too much? Working together and dating at the same time…" She bit back the thought that he and Denae had managed it. That hadn't turned out so well, either, after all.

Leo shifted in his seat, as if thinking the same thing.

She slowed just a hair as she followed the curve of the exit.

"Mia stood up for you and tried to get Vance to accept your abilities for what they are. That was her choice. I did the same thing. He just…took her doing it differently. And that's on him. The fact that they're still bickering just means there were deeper issues."

Ahead of them, Colton put his phone to his ear.

Leo craned his neck. "Again with the phone calls. This guy talks on his phone more than a teenage girl."

"Teenage girls DM and Snapchat, not *chat* chat."

He scowled at her. "You know what I mean. Plus, why put phone to ear instead of letting it flow through the speaker? Archaic."

Chuckling, Emma pulled to a curb five spots behind where Colton parked. "Shit." She glanced at the street sign nearby. "You see where we are?"

His expression tightened. "The Eighth precinct's three blocks up."

*Maybe you were wrong after all, Emma girl.*

She slouched in her seat, and Leo did the same. But in another few seconds, Colton put his phone down and pulled back onto the street. She waited for two cars to pass before following. Ahead of them, his bright-blue sedan fell in behind a silver SUV, keeping pace with it as it left the precinct behind.

"Leo, you don't think…"

"I don't know what to think." He tightened his seat belt.

She sped up and passed two other cars, bringing them closer to Colton's.

"We need to be ready, but he shouldn't know what your Prius looks like. We need to be ready to intervene if it looks like he's about to…"

Emma nodded, and Leo didn't go on. Now that push came to shove, it seemed that even Leo didn't want to voice the possibility that their supposed teammate was about to pull his gun on a police officer.

The unmarked SUV led all of them well out of the precinct's jurisdiction.

For the next twenty minutes or so of driving, Emma remained silent, and Leo seemed no more inclined to speak, as if the other agent might hear them. When the cars made it into an industrial district, the SUV turned into the gravel lot of a large warehouse. It parked in the far southwest corner, and Colton drove up and parked beside it.

"I'm going to pass the lot by, and we'll circle back on foot." Emma sped up slightly but kept just under the speed limit so as not to attract any attention. But when she glanced sideways at just the right moment, the silhouette of the cop leaving the SUV caught in her headlights. "Shit, Leo, that's Brooks Ebenstein!"

"What the hell is the chief doing here?" Leo scowled. "And shit, they've seen us. Jig's up."

Emma dipped her foot onto the gas and swerved, parking on the street just past where Ebenstein and Colton had frozen to watch them. "Then let's get face to face." She was out of the car a second behind Leo but shouting even before her partner came around the side of her Prius. "Colton!"

The other agent grabbed his gun in surprise, but didn't raise it to aim as Emma approached. She hovered her own hand near her holster, her breath coming hard. Leo moved at her side, just as tense. Meanwhile, Ebenstein had backed toward his vehicle, but stood observing them rather than saying anything.

As soon as Colton recognized them, he dropped his gun to his side. "Whatever you're doing here—"

"We're here for answers, Colton." Leo glanced at Ebenstein but then refocused on Colton and moved a step closer. "Whatever you're up to, you need to come clean about it. Now."

Colton seemed to relax. He holstered his gun, shaking his

head. "I should've known you two would magically come out of the woodwork."

Ebenstein's face pinched with concern. "Agent Ambrose, Agent Last—"

"Not now, Chief." Leo's voice was so hard, it didn't sound like him.

"Give us a few seconds, Chief, please." Emma spoke more evenly than Leo, and that, more than anything, seemed to lessen the tension in the air.

Even as she barreled forward, Ebenstein's mouth opened, as if he meant to interrupt, but no sound came out.

"Agent Wright...Colton. What Leo means is that you've been acting strangely for someone who's supposed to be on our team. We also have a mug shot from an arrest Gorik made, our second victim, and I've got to tell you, it's pretty clear to both of us and Jacinda that the face in the mug shot is yours, even if the name is Rick Dwyer. We need to know what's going on."

Colton blanched as he turned to the chief.

"I had to give them Gorik's files, Colton. All of them." Ebenstein coughed, appearing uncomfortable for the first time since Emma first met him. "I want this guy caught."

Sparing him a fast glare, Colton turned back to Leo and Emma. "I can explain."

"I hope so." Emma moved forward, putting herself between Leo and their mystery agent. "I really, really hope so."

## 22

Emma stared at Agent Colton Wright, ignoring the other men on scene. "What the hell were you doing, following the chief? Or any cop, for that matter?"

He looked at Ebenstein. "Chief, would you—"

"Say no more." The chief sighed, glancing around at all of them. "I'll give you folks some privacy. Knock on the window if you need me."

Once he'd gotten back into his driver's seat and slammed the door, Colton nodded, mostly to himself. "Okay, yes, I lied about joining the team to help with the investigation. Or at least, I wasn't completely honest, as that was my cover. I certainly planned to help wherever the chance arose, regardless."

Leo let out a heavy breath. "Get to it, Colton. Why were you added to the team?"

"To watch all of you." He shrugged helplessly, the barest expression of embarrassment crossing his face. "An FBI internal investigation committee put me on you. They suspect your team of having something to do with both the Salem situation and the Hank Barnaby case, though I think the Salem chaos is their primary concern. But the chief called me here to discuss the Gorik link."

*Of course, the higher-ups haven't let the Salem thing go. Even after Jacinda went before fucking Congress.*

Emma shifted her jacket on her shoulders, holding back a curse of frustration that wouldn't help a damned thing. "Salem, okay…things couldn't be weirder around that case, and we all know it. But why's anyone finding something suspicious about the Hank Barnaby case? Any of you can read the files and see how we caught him. It was a clean collar, so what's the issue?"

"With Barnaby, Emma, yeah. All's aboveboard there." Colton stuffed his hands into his pockets, his cheeks appearing pinched even in the dim illumination offered by the streetlights and the chief's taillights. "But there's still no clarity on who was paying him off, and it doesn't look great that we've got two unresolved cases that your team was at the center of, especially considering we have victims from this new case who are from the same precinct as the last."

Leo scoffed. "I hate to say it's a coincidence, but so far, there's no sign to the contrary."

"I know." Colton nodded, his gaze moving between them. "Look, what you should know is that I don't think you've done anything wrong at this point. In fact, I'm doing what I can to clear the team's reputation with the committee. I hoped meeting Ebenstein here and getting his perspective on how the last case went would help with that. Hell, I even went up to Salem, but I came up dry. Obviously, something weird happened there, but there's no evidence suggesting your team was culpable for any wrongdoing."

Some of the tension had left Colton's body since he'd begun clearing the air. His hands came back out of his pockets, hanging loose by his sides, and his expression was more open…no longer showing any sign that he might be hiding anything from them.

Emma glanced at Leo to see if he was reading the man like she was. That he was honest and uncomfortable…but finally telling the truth. From the annoyed but non-defensive look on Leo's face, she guessed he felt the same.

Relief flooded her system, and she managed a small smile. "It's good to hear you're coming around to our way of thinking, Colton. Is it just a matter of you writing a report and the committee signing off?"

The newest member of their team paced over to his car and leaned on the back bumper with a frustrated sigh. "I wish. I've been investigating for weeks, and the committee wants progress. For some reason, my superiors are breathing down my neck and demanding evidence tying your team to what's gone wrong lately."

They all paused as a vehicle passed by on the street. Not a dark-green RAV4 or anything else suspicious. Just someone headed somewhere else.

"The bullet that killed Greg Darby belonging to a stolen gun from Salem won't help your cause, I'm afraid." Colton scrubbed a hand through his hair, adding to its greasiness. "And I thought they were impartial, but it's become clear that's not the case, and it doesn't help that I never felt entirely sure why I was on this case, given how forthcoming everyone's been."

"Jacinda especially." Leo frowned, crossing his arms. "It's not like she wanted to spend days away from the Bureau, catering to questions on Capitol Hill. But at least we know why you've been disappearing and acting so strangely. You're not so great at undercover work, ya know?"

"Ha." Colton straightened up some. "Watch me on a different case, and you'll eat your words. Compared to working with criminals, it's a lot harder to lie to fellow agents who you want on your side."

Emma had to force a smile, because, even as he came clean to them, they were most definitely keeping secrets from him.

She'd spent enough time holding back truths while working with her team. The idea of continuing to do so with Colton...well, it sucked. He'd passed every question they'd thrown, and she still couldn't be honest with him.

Plus, his superiors hadn't been entirely wrong about her being responsible for Salem.

The guilt roiling in her gut reminded her that, in some fashion, she was absolutely culpable. Maybe she hadn't asked for any of it to happen, but if she'd never been born, a lot of people would still be alive, and a whole city might not be reeling from a near apocalypse.

Whether or not Colton thought she was totally innocent, and even went so far as to defend her, she knew the truth. Not that she—or anyone on the team—could admit it.

The ugly feelings stiffened her, but she fought them down and tried to refocus on what Leo and Colton had begun talking about.

"It's me in the mug shot, yeah." Colton half grinned, appearing to loosen up now that he thought everything was out in the open. He brushed a hand over his dark-blond hair, straightening up the mess, suddenly adopting an air of pride. "I was undercover for weeks, investigating a weapons-trade operation, but I'd only just gotten in good with the group when Gorik came along to interrupt things. He arrested me while I was running an errand."

"Not knowing you were undercover," Leo supplied.

He nodded. "But things went off the rails after that. After I got arrested, the traders didn't want anything to do with me, so I got cut loose, and it didn't matter that the charges were dropped. My undercover assignment went up in smoke."

Emma held up a hand to stop him. "Wait, so you didn't have anything to do with Gorik dropping the case?"

"Not a thing." He shrugged. "I didn't even realize Gorik dropped the investigation until a few days ago. Seemed like he was digging deeper and deeper while I was in custody. Knowing what I know now…I can't prove it, but I seriously suspect the person who was running the weapons trade paid Gorik off. That's the only rationale I can come up with for the way the case disappeared. Ebenstein told me he considered it a cold case versus dropped because the trail went cold, but I'm not sure exactly what happened."

Emma tried to keep any bitterness out of her tone. "And you had a new assignment anyway."

"Right." Colton nodded, though his lips were pulled into a frown. "It wasn't my case after I got pulled. The committee brought me in for your team but sent me up to Salem to investigate there first. I told them replacing Denae Monroe after all this time wasn't a good cover, but I got overridden. And like Leo here said, things didn't go as planned. Big lesson learned. I'm too uncomfortable lying to agents as opposed to criminals, so you'd better believe this'll be the last time I take an internal-investigation assignment if I can help it."

Emma didn't disagree with that.

He yawned and waved toward the chief's car. "You both know what I'm here about now. And so do I, so if there are no more questions…"

Leo nodded. "I don't see why not. If he can tell you anything that might make your higher-ups happy, all the better. We don't have anything to hide about how our team handled the case."

Colton straightened from the car. He held his hand out to Leo. "Truce, then? We're on the same team?"

Nodding, Leo reached out and gripped the man's hand, shaking it hard. Emma offered her own hand next, and with the shake, some of the guilt and anxiety running through her bled into exhaustion.

Situation defused.

Secrets kept.

And still no more answers than before they'd followed him.

But the fact that the case Gorik was on went cold so suddenly was certainly suspicious. And with all that money in Gorik's phone wallet, it seemed like their suspicions about him being dirty were more than justified.

*But those layers aren't yet getting us to a killer, Emma girl.*

Walking back to her Prius, Emma took a quick glance at the clock on her phone. Nearing a quarter past eleven already. She got in and glanced Leo's way as he slammed his door. "You think it's too late to text someone and ask about a late-night visit?"

His eyebrow rose as she started the Prius. "Not if they're a friend, and it's important. Or are you talking about the case?"

Emma shook her head, pulling up her psychic's number. "No, I'm thinking of Marigold."

"Text her." Leo shrugged. "If she doesn't answer, she doesn't answer."

Emma typed out a quick message, asking if the psychic was awake, and if she was, if she'd put up with a late-night visit.

Marigold's reply was almost instantaneous. *I just finished a late session, so I'm wide awake. Come on over. I'll have tea ready.*

Relaxing into her seat, Emma tucked her phone away. "She's up. I'll head over there from the Bureau." She did a U-turn and headed back to HQ to drop Leo off.

Leo nodded, apparently as tired as she was, since he didn't bother to reply.

For her part, Emma allowed the night's discoveries to wash over her as she considered how to approach the topic of a possible sibling.

The lack of answers had begun weighing on her more and more, and now her survivor's guilt was only making things worse.

If she went home now, she'd never sleep.

*Maybe you're not meant to, Emma girl. Maybe the guilty shouldn't sleep.*

Emma flinched, biting her lip. She knew what Leo would say to that thought, as well as the sudden doubts she'd had earlier…but her inner voice was only telling her the truth.

## 23

Lydia put me on hold, so I took the opportunity to tuck the binoculars back into their case. The agents were long gone. I had to admit, I'd been skeptical about this part of the plan, but it had paid off in spades.

My baby girl had been right.

Watching those agents get confrontational and transmitting the whole video to Lydia so that we could have the pleasure of watching this team fall apart…heaven. We were going to sleep well tonight.

As the two agents disappeared down the road, the intoxication of the moment settled in my bones and gave me the extra strength I needed for my baby. She liked me focused on her at all times, and now I had the energy for it.

In the darkness of the car, I sipped from my water bottle and waited. With things progressing as they were, I had no reason to hurry.

"Are you still there?" She came back on the line.

"Of course."

That chuckling sounded out again. "I knew you could do it. You can do anything with the right attitude."

I swallowed, tamping down the thrill running through my blood. She didn't outright compliment me often. "It was your planning that was perfect."

*Perfect* was an understatement. What had sounded pretty insane and reckless appeared to be going just as she'd predicted it would.

"Yes, I guess it was." She was all breathy. "But you've done…okay…so far." She paused, her breath seeming heavier, angrier. *Damn, she can switch on a dime.* "What's important now is that even if all the agents are all on the same side now, we still have to keep your head on a swivel."

I grinned. "Yes, ma'am." I submitted to her "orders," or at least led her to believe I did.

Because I was about to let this city know just what I was made of. And I was going to do it with her, but I would still go it alone if I had to…

## 24

Emma arrived at Marigold's home right around midnight, and the older woman had the door open even as she approached the front stoop. "Marigold, I'm so sorry to call so late."

Smiling, the psychic pulled Emma into a quick motherly hug. The flowery smell of her hair was so familiar and comforting, Emma felt as if she'd just walked into a childhood memory.

"Stop apologizing." Marigold pushed the door open wider. "You think I would've told you to come over if I hadn't meant it? Come sit down and tell me what's going on."

In her reading room, surrounded by dark built-ins with books galore, Emma wrapped her hands around the large mug of mint and chamomile tea. The smell was unspeakably relaxing. The more she got used to this space, the more Emma felt safe there, despite the unfamiliarity of the crystals laid out on Marigold's reading table tonight.

When the psychic settled at the table across from her, a mug of tea in her own hands, Emma swallowed…then dove in without preamble. "We talked about what happened in Salem, but remember how we got cut off?"

Marigold nodded, gesturing her on.

That'd been one of the many conversations Emma was forced to interrupt because of a work call. "Well, what I didn't get a chance to tell you is that Celeste had some dying words for me."

Marigold's brow knit. "Not an apology or final regrets, I suppose?"

Emma nearly spit her tea out with the little laugh that escaped. "I wish. No. She mentioned that I have a sister. And I know, I know, she was probably messing with me…but I can't help thinking maybe she wasn't."

Marigold nodded, that perceptive gaze remaining tight on Emma's. "I imagine that would be difficult to put out of mind. And from the look on your face, that's not all."

Another sip of tea calmed Emma's rising pulse somewhat, but it was too late to stop now. "And…I've been feeling a lot of guilt over what happened. All those people would be alive if not for me. Even Celeste Foss."

Marigold reached across the table and rested her hand lightly on Emma's. "All the loss you've experienced, with your parents, you should be able to recognize survivor's guilt. It's a hard thing, but you know you cannot hold yourself responsible."

Suddenly, Emma thought she might cry. She held the emotion back, though, blinking it away. "Survivor's guilt" felt too pedestrian a term when it came to dozens of deaths. Finally, though, she nodded. "I understand what you're saying, at least logically. Difference between brain and heart, you know? I'm trying to get past it. But…well…there's more."

Marigold frowned. "Of course there is. There always is, due to your experiences with the Other. Keep going."

"The bullets collected as evidence in the latest case…" Emma clenched her tea mug tighter and waited until a shiver passed. "One of them was fired from a gun Celeste stole from the Salem PD armory. The other bullet isn't back from ballistics, but it's going to be a match, I know it."

Marigold's eyes were serious. "It sounds like you're right to suspect these crimes are linked to you, and that someone is trying very hard to scare you. Or worse."

Emma let her gaze focus on the bowl of small crystals at the center of the table, forcing herself to keep going. "If Celeste wasn't lying, and I really do have a sister out there who's out for revenge, do you think she could be behind this? I don't have any reason to suspect her, specifically, but I don't have any reason not to."

As she waited for Marigold to contradict her, her throat constricted when the other woman nodded.

"I suppose it would make sense. If there's a daughter out there, grieving the loss of her mother, she could blame you, especially if she possesses her mother's…disposition."

"I was afraid you'd say that." Emma sighed, her mind racing with the implications. Was she about to be hunting her own sister, or was she doing so already? "And I have to say, it's all making me pretty paranoid. My team…well, I can't go into too much detail, but we're still hunting for a killer. And he might even be a member of the Bureau, based on what little we know. But…I'm floundering, it feels like, especially with this new evidence about where the bullet came from that killed the first officer. I need answers, or I might just drown in…"

She cut herself off before her emotions got the best of her.

Marigold leaned forward. "Drown in what, Emma dear?"

"Guilt!" Emma choked out. "Every time I start to believe it's in the past, and I can rebuild, it starts piling up again."

Marigold gripped her forearm. "You need to slow down."

"That's just it!" Emma found herself nearly panting for breath, the emotions of the last few days suddenly building. "I can't slow down! We have a killer on the loose."

Marigold stared at her hard and held her arm tighter. "Emma, honey, now that I know you, I know there's *always* a killer on the loose. You have to take care of yourself before you can catch up to them, though. So slow down, okay? Deep breaths."

*That's just what Oren would say.*

Emma could almost see him standing behind Marigold. Arms crossed, his flyaway hair surrounding that calm, understanding face she'd been falling in love with before he died. Him there in his yoga attire, as strong as he was relaxed. Telling her to breathe.

The way she missed him…it sometimes seemed unfair that she couldn't make him real. Couldn't simply speak to him whenever she wanted, even with her ability.

Yet…

She shook herself from the vision, met Marigold's gaze, and forced herself to nod.

The psychic's eyes narrowed, and she observed her for another moment before she continued. "Did you see something just then? Here?"

Emma sucked on her lower lip before answering, centering herself. "Just thinking of Oren."

Marigold observed her for another moment, smiling gently. "Okay, just take those good, deep breaths. You keep thinking of Oren, since he centers you like that."

*That much I can do.*

"First of all, you need to get it through your thick skull that *you are not responsible for what happened in Salem*. You hear me? I'm sure being stubborn is an asset in your line of work, but for the sake of your sanity, you must accept that."

Marigold watched her, seemingly waiting, then nodded. "Repeat it. You are not responsible for Salem."

Emma took another deep breath. Then another. "I am not responsible for what happened in Salem." The words almost felt true, as long as she kept breathing deeply.

"Good girl. And you keep repeating that out loud as often as you need to. Remember, you've dealt with crippling grief before, and that was not your fault. But grief will push you to crumble if you allow it to. Celeste was responsible for all that destruction and death. Hell, you stopped her! You and your team. If not for you, many more people would've died."

Emma took a sip of her tea, then forced herself back to the thought that kept arguing with what Marigold had just said. "But, Marigold, if I'd never been born—"

"Celeste would still have been born." Marigold's voice turned stern. She reached to the bowl of crystals and pushed a blue mineral chunk into Emma's hands. "You hold this apatite and listen to me, Emma. Celeste would've been born, even if you hadn't. And if she had the capacity for such evil inside her, which she did, it would've found its way out, which it did. But without you, there'd have been nobody to stop her."

Emma inhaled deeply, fingering the stone in her hands. Somehow, Marigold's words sounded irrefutable. She glanced at the crystal, then at the ring on Marigold's right middle finger. The stones seemed to match.

Marigold twisted her ring, smiling. "I practice what I preach, Emma."

"Did you just brainwash me into believing you?"

The other woman barked a laugh. "Not likely. But I think you should keep that gemstone on you. Apatite is a stone that represents and reinforces truth, as well as confidence. Psychics use it sometimes to find equilibrium for overactive energy centers. It can also stimulate energy centers when necessary…think of it as a psychic energy backup. Your self-doubt is acting up something fierce, and this stone could help you keep your mental clarity. Promise me you'll keep it on you?"

Emma turned the stone around and around, which was small enough to fit in her pocket without being noticeable, smaller than an acorn. "I'll do my best."

Marigold didn't seem pleased with the noncommitment. "If it's an added incentive, that same stone is sometimes used to connect with higher realms. Like the Other."

Emma jerked her gaze up, her grip on the crystal tightening.

Marigold smiled, her body relaxing in what appeared to be relief. "I thought that might do it. It's true, of course, but anything to keep you holding on to your confidence is worth something."

"Thank you." Emma rubbed the stone as she sipped her tea, and it almost seemed to warm with the words. "Speaking of the Other…I was wondering if we could do another séance."

Marigold's entire being shifted, and she lifted her tea to her lips, clearly giving herself a moment to think. "Emma, I'm not—"

"It could shed some light on whether my sister could be behind this, or if she even exists."

Marigold licked her lips before shaking her head. "You don't need me for this. You have everything you need to know."

"No, I don't!" Emma barked the words much louder than she'd intended. "Sorry."

"It's okay. Just…think. Do you have a sister? Have you ever felt or seen anything to indicate that?"

Emma breathed out and sat back in her chair. "No. I would know if my mother had had another child. She practically would've been a child. And she died shortly after I was born. So no." She shook her head.

"So maybe Celeste was speaking figuratively."

"The room!" Emma could see it clearly. "The pink girl's bedroom in Celeste's home. I was in it before it went up in flames." Did Celeste have a child, despite putting a curse on Gina—her own mother—for doing so?

"And…" Marigold nudged her along.

Emma squeezed the stone for support. "Celeste saw Gina and Monique as sisters. Maybe she meant her child and me were then 'sisters' too."

"Could be."

"Maybe my mother and Celeste were actually related somehow in real life."

Marigold shrugged. "I think you're on the right track about Celeste having a child."

Emma kept the rest of her theories to herself as she pocketed the apatite and stood. "Thank you so much. This stone…I really appreciate it."

Marigold pushed herself to her feet, bracing herself on the table. "You're more than welcome. And you stay in touch. I'm glad to help however I can. You're not alone in this."

Emma moved around the table and gave the woman a firm hug, relishing the contact and warmth.

*I'm not alone. I have to remember that.*

In seconds, she found herself walking out to her car, the psychic's door locking behind her. The night somehow felt colder and darker than it had earlier, and Emma picked up the pace.

Nerves ran heavy in her blood as she fingered the little crystal. It had felt more useful in the calm space of Marigold's reading room. Out in the dark and the cold, it was more like a poor person's weapon, but she supposed it couldn't hurt.

*What would it mean, Emma girl, if this sister is also of Celeste's blood?*

If the crazed woman's dying words were more than a threat, it only meant one thing. And Emma wasn't ready to face that.

## 25

With the glare of the morning sun slicking into the garage, Emma pulled into a spot near Leo's truck just as he emerged from the cab. She nodded in the direction of Colton's shiny blue TLX as they began walking toward the elevator together.

Leo sighed, though his lips were already trained in a smile. "What timing, huh?"

Colton was out of his vehicle, slamming the door a second later. The other agent appeared to have been waiting for them.

"Good morning." Emma felt some tension ease out of her shoulders at seeing how relaxed Colton appeared.

He nodded but looked apprehensive. "I'm not about to get the third degree again, am I? Because you were walking over here like a woman on a mission."

Leo laughed. "She always is."

Emma fought the urge to roll her eyes. "Well, now that I've slept on our conversation, I do have a few more questions. Do you mind?"

He raised an eyebrow. "I'm assuming that's rhetorical."

"Touché." She shifted her bag on her shoulder, rethinking how to phrase it. "You told us briefly about the case you were undercover on, where Gorik arrested you, but only in broad strokes. What did you learn while you were under?"

"Oh, that." He ran a hand through his hair. "Honestly, I spoke in so-called broad strokes because I didn't learn much. The organization I got in with was very secretive, and it was probably a miracle I got assigned an errand as fast as I did. But I wasn't around long enough to build the trust I'd have needed to know who was pulling the strings."

"Shit." Emma was disappointed, and even then wondered if the agent was telling her the truth. "So much for that thought."

Leo nodded toward the elevator, tapping his watch, and the three of them started walking.

Moving in step with Emma, Colton went on. "Look, I'm sorry I didn't tell you I knew Gorik. When his body was first discovered, I mean. But with all the stress I was under, I didn't even recognize him at first. It was like I said, the committee had called me in."

*We were accusing him of murder, and here he was just trying to balance two different cases. Nice.*

Emma jabbed the button for the elevator. "Colton, forget the case for a second. How will this committee respond to the fact that your cover's blown? I assume you plan to tell them?"

He shrugged. "Honestly…I feel too invested in this case to disappear from the team now. So I'd just as soon let the committee bide their time waiting on me. My plan is to tell them as soon as the case is over, which means we'd better solve it quick."

Leo shook his head as they entered the elevator. "You don't think they'll catch on if they touch base with Jacinda and hear the dynamic's shifted? Or even before that, when they learn Freddy Gorik is our second victim? Someone will connect the dots like we have."

He shrugged again. "You all can keep treating me with suspicion if you want. That might help." A chuckle bubbled out of him for the first time, making him appear years younger. "But I informed them this morning that you two are catching wind of me being here as an interdivisional spy, so they ought to back off until I come to them with answers. I don't think they'll pull me in any case, not with the first bullet tracing back to a stolen Salem PD gun. And meanwhile, we can work together. I'll do what I can to assist."

"And if we solve this," Emma spoke fast, as the elevator was nearly to the VCU headquarters, "all the fucking cop killers on our radar will find themselves behind bars, you'll be able to help clear the team in the eyes of the FBI, and we can all move on."

"Let's hope so." Colton grinned, and he was the first to step out of the elevator. Already, he seemed to move with more confidence than yesterday, betraying the fact that acting as a spy really was weighing on him.

Emma nudged Leo with her elbow. "All good?"

He nodded, mumbling a reply in the affirmative. The sheepish expression on his face was confirmation enough, though.

Finally, they had everyone on the same page, with one intention only.

To catch a killer.

Emma slipped a hand into her pocket and rubbed one finger along the apatite Marigold had given her. Was this innocuous little gem part of the reason she wasn't feeling debilitating doubt?

She certainly hadn't gotten enough sleep to use that as the reason, but somehow, she felt like they might finally be moving forward. At some point, she might even have to ask Marigold if she had any other tricks up her sleeve. Real, psychosomatic, Other-based tricks or even plain old wives' tales...she'd take anything that worked.

All the better if it helped her zero in on crooks—or the so-called sister who might actually exist.

The thought of being biologically linked to someone connected to Celeste sat like a stone in her gut. More than once, she'd woken in the middle of the night drenched in sweat, heart pounding. One dream stuck with her—the worst of them.

She was sitting at a table, staring at an old family photo of her and her parents. But there, at the edge of the frame, half shadowed and watching, was Celeste.

*In* the picture.

Because if this sister was real—and if she was related to Celeste by blood—then that meant Celeste had been family too. In some twisted, tangential, unbearable way.

And Emma had killed her.

What would her sister think of that?

Was *that* what this was all about?

## 26

Emma mostly observed Jacinda as Agent Colton Wright laid out the truth for the whole team. The SSA's expression, purse-lipped and narrow-eyed, might best have been described as resigned, so Emma guessed she'd suspected as much already.

When her gaze flicked to Emma's, apparently having felt the weight of observation, Emma shifted in her seat and did her best to appear interested in her new colleague. But since she'd already heard his story, she couldn't help but watch everyone else take it in.

Pointedly, everyone around the conference table was focused solely on Colton—especially Vance—but nobody looked particularly surprised by his true purpose.

To his credit, he gave a good briefing, offering everything up in a logical fashion that answered questions just as they might arise naturally. And he seemed more comfortable than he had since she'd met him, even in a room of people he'd been sent to spy on.

When he finished and offered to answer any further questions, nobody took him up on it.

Jacinda motioned for him to take a seat, and Emma didn't waste any time leaning forward with what remained foremost on her mind. "I think there's a potential connection between Colton's undercover case and the crimes. If Gorik really did get paid off by a weapons dealer, that's the logical place for us to search out whoever blackmailed him."

Colton nodded. "The more I think about it, the more I agree. Not that I saw any sign of a killer in the organization, but given the amount of secrecy, I have to believe folks within that fold would be capable."

"It could've been someone within the organization." Jacinda nodded, pulling her hair back behind her shoulders. "Or it could simply have been someone close enough to know about the bribe…whether close enough to the person who did the bribing or the organization as a whole. But I agree that's the best way to move forward."

Vance turned his focus to Colton. "Do you have any contacts left in the organization? Someone who might be willing to talk to you based on your undercover persona?"

Sitting back in his seat, Colton considered the question, his eyes going a little unfocused. "There might be one person. I can't guarantee until I talk to him, but he was trying to work his way up, just like I was. I don't know if I've ever seen such a…such a professionally minded organization. Everyone vying for recognition and status."

Leo jotted something down in his notebook. "How's that different from any other organized criminal entity?"

"I think of people making their way into most gangs or criminal groups via the edges, watching to see how things go, and getting a foot in where they can *as* they can, but mostly taking things as they come. With the Cloaks? Not so much."

The Cloaks? They were a clandestine operation, that was for sure. But what little Emma knew of them correlated with what Colton was saying.

"No lazybones?" Mia tried to joke, but Colton's dire frown stilled her and Emma both.

"You have no idea." He fidgeted with his tie. "There were rumors about how screwups got dealt with. I wasn't in a position to verify anything, but we're not talking about guys just getting kicked out on the street. We're talking silenced permanently even if the screwup was what we'd call minor. Compare it to showing up late to the office by fifteen minutes and getting docked a month's pay for the first-time offense."

When Leo whistled, Jacinda shot him a look before turning back to Colton. "Which means any interaction with this organization needs to be well-thought-out. Tell us about this guy."

"He's a foot soldier." Colton loosened his tie, stretching his neck as if he were remembering the man or his own persona already. "We got reasonably chummy since we had different skill sets. We weren't competing so much as trying to achieve the same goal. I could get out of here and try to touch base with him today. Jack Darko's his name."

Vance stopped typing. "Darko? That cannot be his real name. It's like he got that out of a naming app for minions."

Jacinda gave Vance a look to cut the quips. "You're not going alone, Colton." Her flat statement made Colton jolt in his seat. "Undercovers might consider themselves lone wolves, but while you're part of this team, you need backup."

"I'll go with him." Emma ignored Colton's surprised look. "I can pose as a weapon buyer, maybe a woman who needs some extra protection against an ex, and we can ask Darko to hook us up with the best option he's got. If he agrees, we can tail whoever delivers the weapon."

Leo opened his mouth, maybe to protest, but Colton was already agreeing. "It'd be less suspicious if I'm with a woman.

Emma doesn't exactly scream 'agent,' as long as she's not wearing her jacket."

"My street clothes are ready and waiting." Emma raised an eyebrow at Jacinda, and the SSA nodded.

"All right, then that's the plan." Jacinda looked at Mia. "You have street clothes on hand?"

Mia blinked. "Yeah, of course."

"All right, then I want you along as backup. Emma'll wear a wire, and you'll monitor everything in case the two of them need a distraction, more backup, whatever. Colton, see if you can contact this Darko, and then the three of you can change clothes and meet up on his turf."

Colton got up and walked out, turning and gesturing that he'd meet them downstairs in five.

"Meanwhile," Jacinda went on, "the rest of us will keep digging in other directions. I don't want us back at square one if you come up dry. You two start looking into every 'Knight' in the FBI database over the last three decades if you haven't already. There's a reason our unsub used the name Knight before killing both Greg Darby and Freddy Gorik."

Leo nodded. "We'll find it."

"And there's no way there isn't a link with Darby. This can't have been a random act of violence or a case of wrong place, wrong time. Colton didn't find a connection, but it's there." Jacinda looked more at Vance when she stated that, as he seemed to be lost in space.

Vance gave Jacinda a quick glance in the affirmative, but then he rose and reached to catch Mia's elbow as she stood. "Can I talk to you?"

Leo didn't look any happier than Vance, but Emma could tell he was thinking the same thing—right as Mia whispered at Vance, "Back off."

Emma stood abruptly, cutting off the brewing argument before it could erupt. Leo followed suit, a beat too fast.

The sudden movement caught attention. Vance and Mia fell silent, both turning to watch Emma go. She paused, forced a smile, but the moment had already shifted.

The rest of the table began to stir.

In the end, Emma held the door open for Vance and Mia, giving them the perfect excuse to slip off to the breakroom and hash it out in private. Jacinda observed, looking just a breath away from scolding them like a parent before heading back to her office.

Emma hurried to her desk, anxious to review messages and check in with Renee Bailey before getting a move on. She hadn't sat down before the breakroom door slammed.

And it still wasn't enough to keep in the sounds of what followed.

"Everything's changed!" Vance's whisper-yell was loud enough to have made it to Jacinda's office, too, if she hadn't had her door closed. "Ever since you-know-what came out, we're just following her around blindly!"

*At least he's speaking in riddles.*

Colton had disappeared, thankfully, or Emma might've worried about him overhearing, but this was so uncomfortable, she wished she'd gone with him. Leo glanced at her, mouth open in shock, and she dropped into her desk chair.

Mia's voice was nearly as loud. "She's just trying to solve crimes and play the hand she's been dealt. You need to get a grip and do the same."

The sound of a bang echoed out of the room—Vance's fist or boot against a door, Emma guessed.

"Do you even listen to me? You're about to follow her now, on Jacinda's say-so! Did you hear me last night?"

Leo stared at his legal pad and muttered. "I wish I had my headphones. The big-ass ones that cover my whole ears."

But before Emma could reply, Mia had yanked open the

door. Her face was still turned away, though. "I always hear you. Maybe that's the fucking problem!"

*Slam!*

Mia whirled around to the heart of the VCU and stilled for a second on seeing Emma and Leo watching her. Her cheeks went pink, but she kept her shoulders back and chin up. "You ready?"

Emma was already out of her chair. Whatever state Vance came out of that room in, she'd leave Leo to deal with it.

## 27

Leo hadn't worn headphones while working in years. Not since he'd had a teammate who'd insisted on reading his case notes out loud to himself. That distraction had gotten him used to privatizing his hearing fast. But now…

Vance's boot thumped into what Leo guessed was the breakroom refrigerator, again. Jacinda had peeked out when the door had slammed for a third time earlier—after Mia slammed it, Vance had opened it and slammed it again for good measure—but she'd retreated back into her office in seconds. Just as soon as she figured out what was happening, Leo guessed.

Since joining the VCU, he'd never until now wished to all hell that he had his own private office too.

But he couldn't help that, which meant he just needed to focus on the case. Maybe, with any luck, he'd catch a break before Emma and Colton even knocked on this Darko character's door.

He opened the files he'd pulled up the night before—when his eyes had practically been buzzing from overuse.

Just as he was about to get started, the emotion of the early morning came back to him fast, though.

Leo had some idea of the guilt Emma was feeling over the last week or so. It'd hit him as soon as he'd woken up, after a good night's sleep and a healthy helping of crow from the night before.

Never in his whole career did he remember pushing so hard in the wrong direction on a case, but he'd been sure Colton was entangled in the murders.

He didn't like being wrong but was glad he was.

Leo pulled fifty-five names from the database. Seven were deceased. Two were over eighty, and eight were women. That left thirty-eight possibilities of male agents named Knight. Thirty-three of them were active, from the ages of twenty-five to fifty-six. Agents retired at fifty-seven in the FBI, and five of them were between fifty-seven and seventy-six. They weren't discounted, though. Leo would look into all thirty-eight.

*The MPD could be doing this, too, if they had clearance to view agent files, and we'd get this done in double time.*

Glancing up, he caught himself sighing as Vance let out an angry curse on the other side of the door. The man was dealing with the fallout of a relationship, but it wasn't just that. Leo had gone through plenty of emotions himself after Denae had said she "needed time," but at least they'd parted on decent terms. Vance and Mia were self-destructing.

And seeing Emma and Mia go off with a man who might as well be a stranger…that hadn't been easy, even for Leo. Sure, the guy appeared to be an established agent, but just like with other professions, some agents were better than others. Leo would've preferred being her partner if she was going even slightly undercover. Or Colton's partner instead of Emma.

And, realistically, he wanted to contribute something concrete to this damn case. He wanted to be part of this team and get them across the finish line. Especially after barking up the wrong tree so much that Emma and Jacinda would've been totally within their rights to give him *I told you so* lectures three times over. He'd led them astray, they'd been patient with getting him to see who Colton really was, and now it felt like he was being punished with desk duty.

That wasn't it. He knew that. Someone had to be looking into this Agent Knight. He agreed with Jacinda that there had to be a connection, however thin. A clue, however obscure.

But he didn't trust Colton yet. Least of all with his teammates' lives and especially with a criminal organization that, by Colton's own words, viewed being tardy as worthy of the death penalty. These were serious people they were tampering with, and Colton was used to working alone.

People who worked alone didn't necessarily know how to have a partner's back, even if they had the best of intentions.

Maybe the problem was that he'd been trying too hard to come up with the silver bullet in this case. Ever since Emma's ability was made public knowledge—to the team, at least—she seemed to be the one running the show. Not that he felt the resentment Vance did…but he was used to being someone everyone trusted and turned to for immediate answers. Now that was mostly Emma's role.

Leo chastised his own ego and started inputting badge numbers to pull up pictures.

He needed to take every task seriously and get his head out of his ass…even if the current task felt more like busywork than anything useful.

Vance had gone quiet, only breaking his silence seconds later. He barked out a laugh. "And I'm the one she says needs to get a grip! Fuck!"

Leo flinched. That phrase "get a grip" was one his

grandfather had used on him and his brothers when he'd been particularly annoyed. Mia's use of it earlier had been like a hammer to his memories.

As if to confirm the reaction, the slam of the breakroom door sounded out. Vance stomped back into the VCU's main area, and Leo did his best to appear as if he hadn't heard anything, keeping his focus on his computer screen. Across from him, Vance dropped into his seat and tore open a file. Papers fluttered onto the floor. They both ignored them.

Much as Leo wanted to take some comfort in the fact that Vance felt the same way he did about them following Emma a little too blindly, he, too, needed to drop the egocentric bullshit before they both ended up in hot water over it.

Emma's ability was an asset to the team. Hell, it might even be an asset to the world. Time would tell on that account, but he and everyone else who knew about it needed to get on the same page and accept it for what it was. Vance would see that soon.

Leo would just have to swallow his pride and support her, however he could.

*Even if that means endless paperwork.*

The thought made him squirm, but he kept his eyes on the files in front of him. Emma could take care of herself anyway. If she and Colton came up short on this lead, though, he'd damn well make sure he was at the helm of the next plan.

"I'm running through the Knights."

Vance laughed, then cut it short, seeming to remember he was pissed.

Leo gave him a look but kept silent.

"Sounded like that Lionel Richie song."

His irritation was about to bubble up all over again. "I didn't take you for a soft rock guy."

Vance shook his head but didn't bother looking up. "Okay, you've got Knight. How many you down to?"

"A dozen."

"Cool. I'll dig back into Darby, see what Colton might've missed."

*Hopefully, a direct connection to our killer.*

## 28

Mia adjusted her running hoodie and tried to relax. "What's this guy like, Colton?"

Their new teammate met her eyes through the rearview mirror of the Bureau undercover vehicle, an old Toyota, and she forced a smile. She'd done her best to put the argument with Vance behind her when she'd changed clothes, but it wasn't that simple. The man was being insufferable—which he'd been for some time—and every moment she tried to think of anything *but* their relationship, Vance had to go and remind her he was an overbearing, impatient, paranoid horse's ass.

It was a lot.

And Colton's perceptive gaze seemed to read most of that in her expression, even as Emma contented herself with studying the world outside the window.

"Darko's smart in the way of criminals. Ambitious, so I think he'll have made headway in the organization. But at heart, he's a criminal. He's cagey but won't be asking us a bunch of questions. Emma and I can say we met at a gym, and he'll be content with that."

Emma hummed agreement from beside him. Dressed in a black crewneck thermal and jeans and fully at ease. Unlike Mia.

Colton turned left down a run-down suburban street. Wearing a muscle shirt and sweatpants, he certainly looked the part of a gym rat, all muscles and hard edges. He had a hoodie, but something told Mia he wouldn't be putting it on. "Taking each other's leads should be more than enough for us to get by, but…"

"But what?" Mia wanted to throttle the words out of him. What was wrong with the men in her life? "What are you not telling us?"

"Nothing." Colton grinned, but there was something else behind the expression. "But your attitude is…"

"What?" Mia nearly shouted but managed to keep it to a dull roar.

Emma visibly flinched in the passenger seat.

Cursing Vance mentally, she shook her head. "Sorry. There's a lot going on with…me and my boyfriend. I won't let it affect me, promise."

"I think it should." Colton squinted at her through the mirror, and Emma finally turned from the window.

"What'd you just say?"

Colton shrugged before pulling into a small parking lot across from the entrance to an apartment complex. "Emma, you told me to be straight with you. I'm being straight now. Mia's all wound up about her boyfriend, and that's exactly the attitude we need. You're calm as a computer in sleep mode. She'd be perfect."

Emma's mouth dropped open in surprise, and Mia blinked. "You want me to take Emma's place?"

"No." Emma undid her seat belt and glanced between them, a hard set to her jaw. "This isn't what we planned—"

"But it makes sense." Colton stretched his arms above his

head, intertwined fingers hitting the car roof and stretching behind him. If Vance had seen his muscles flexing while he proposed what he did, his head would've exploded. "Mia's primed for the job, and you're not. She's just as capable, right?"

"Yes." Mia undid her seat belt and met Emma's surprised gaze.

Colton grinned.

"Emma, it might make more sense."

Emma grimaced. "This isn't just dangerous. This is—"

"An op." Colton shrugged, that maddening grin coming back. He was getting into character, Mia realized. Loosening up his muscles and his attitude both. "Let's get it done already. Ask Jacinda if you need to, but this is what makes sense, and you know it."

Emma swallowed hard, and Mia could see her brain swimming. But what she'd said was true. Emma was always the one running off half-cocked, pretending to be someone else in order to open a door or speed after a criminal. Mia was more often babysitting suspects or questioning witnesses who were more likely to cry than pull out a gun. Unless she was side by side with Emma or the rest of the team, at least.

*Vance would so hate this.*

"Colton's right. I'm doing it." Before Emma could argue, Mia pulled the earbud from her ear and handed it to Emma. "Take it. Give me the wire. You drop Jacinda a text to let her know the change of plans. She'll understand. And then we'll sound-check this and get it done."

Emma ran her tongue along her teeth, visibly annoyed, but then she fished the wire out from beneath her thermal and passed it into the back seat. "You want me to tell Vance too?" Her thumb flew over her phone screen as she texted Jacinda.

"Ha." Mia took the wire and dropped it into her running hoodie. She used the clip to hold the mic to the middle of her bra, adding tape for extra security. "Do whatever you think makes sense."

Colton grinned at her, appearing easy and free, and a rush of adrenaline sped through Mia's nerves. She hadn't felt this excited about life in...

*Don't think like that. Don't bring Vance into it. Get your head on straight.*

*Now.*

Emma's phone rang. She flashed the screen at them before hitting Accept. It was Jacinda.

"Jacinda, hi. I have you on speak—"

"It's not happening." Fury punctuated each syllable.

"Jacinda." Mia's eyes went wide. "Colton and I agree that I'd be the better choice."

"Because you've been a volatile teenage ball of emotions all day? You and Vance are lucky you're not sitting in opposite corners of the breakroom in a time-out."

"That's why we think I'd be perfect!"

"It's Emma, final answer. Or I'm pulling the whole op."

Mia opened her mouth to argue but forced it closed, angry to her bones. Emma, however, seemed to be working really hard to keep a neutral face. Mia at least hoped she was.

"Got it, Jacinda. We'll check in when it's over." Emma hung up.

Mia reluctantly undid the wire and handed it over to Emma, who put it back in place inside her shirt, hooking it to her bra.

Mia wanted to pummel her damn boyfriend, who, in her opinion, just blew this chance for her.

Nonetheless, she came around the car once they all got out and gave Emma a quick hug, whispering for her to be safe. And she meant it. It wasn't her going in, but she didn't know what she'd do without Emma as a partner or friend.

What if Darko's apartment was swimming in other Cloaks members and they were caught totally unawares? She gave Colton a nod but directed a small smile Emma's way that told her to be careful.

Mia stepped back around to the driver's side door.

Colton had his hands propped partially in his pockets. "Okay, Emma. You ready to be vulnerable?"

Emma stared up at the handsome agent with the Hollywood good looks and the grating personality, and she hooked an arm around one of his sculpted biceps. "Screw you, Colton. I'm gonna play this my way." She leaned into him, cozying up nice and tight.

And just like that, they started across the street, as Mia got back in the car and slouched down in the driver's seat.

It felt incredibly odd to be teaming up with a man who, less than twenty-four hours ago, the team had thought might be a murderer.

She just hoped they were right in trusting that he wasn't.

## 29

"You must've been chummy." Emma flipped her hair as she gazed up at Colton. She'd definitely look like his girlfriend to anybody setting eyes on them. "For you to know where he lives, I mean."

"Memory of an elephant is all." Colton tapped his head.

His muscles had coiled like a snake the moment she touched him, and he hadn't relaxed yet. She gave him a little pinch on the underside of his upper arm, the kind that stung.

"Hey!" He added a laugh, but his eyes told her she'd pay for that.

"Somebody needs to loosen up." She shook his arm and batted her lashes at him. "Now, breathe and tell me about this guy."

Colton took a beat, but then he relaxed. "I had to get the guy home once after he had a few too many drinks. He's a nice guy, really, but not the brightest. The old number I had for him didn't work, like I said, but we'll try his place first. Failing that, I know a few of his old hangouts where we might have luck."

It was coming up on ten in the morning. If the guy didn't

have a regular job—and weapons dealers didn't generally follow the nine-to-five clock—odds were they'd find him at home. She agreed with Colton on that much.

Emma glanced about, ensuring nobody was near enough to hear before she asked her next question. Around them, the apartment complex was silent but for a passing SUV. "I know you weren't in the organization long, but what did you do specifically while you were in? I feel like I would know that about you."

He shrugged. "Mostly deliveries. Nothing big. We're talking a paper bag with a gun versus a truckload. Everyone above me was too careful for me to learn much. Whoever was importing the weapons didn't want anything traced back to them, clearly. The person in charge would drop off packages with instructions about where to take them, but since they chose the drop spots and used a different one every time, it wasn't possible to set up surveillance in advance, and no matter how fast I moved on an order, I never caught sight of them."

"And you were trying to build trust, anyway, so I imagine you were following orders pretty closely."

"Exactly." Colton slowed his pace just a touch, reflecting the serious tone that had just slipped into his voice. "And to be truthful, if they'd caught me tailing anyone after a drop-off, it would've gotten me killed, gotten 'Rick Dwyer' killed. I sugarcoated how serious they are. Showing up to a meeting late might've gotten me a beating. Me tailing anyone? Someone would've slit my throat."

"If that's the case, why's approaching Darko going to be any different? I mean, not that it's a screwup, but it's out of the ordinary. If this guy comes through, the person doing the drop-off might see us tailing them and recognize you."

Colton shook his head. "I'm a nobody, as far as these guys go. But, yeah, my face could get recognized, so it won't be me. Your boy Leo didn't exactly look thrilled when you and Mia were singled out to accompany me. I'm guessing he'd jump at the chance to take my place and stick around for the stakeout. He and Vance or whoever can tail him."

"You're pretty new to the team. Even in the best of circumstances, there might've been some nerves around one of us going undercover with you."

"Just means you all watch each other's backs. That's a good thing."

*And each other's secrets too. But we'll leave that for another day, if ever.*

The dingy apartment complex took up an entire city block. The maze of gray-blue buildings didn't seem to offer any street signs, and the numbers on the units were small enough to have been designed for confusion.

Emma dictated the turns they were taking to Mia, diligent about the minor landmarks they passed. An Irish flag on one corner, a toddler-size garden gnome on another. If Mia needed to barge in like the proverbial calvary, she'd know how to find them.

When Colton stopped in front of a four-story unit that looked just like the rest, Emma stared at him hard enough that he laughed. "You grow up in a labyrinth like this, you learn to remember how to navigate them."

She shook her head and leaned into him even more, playing the clingy girlfriend just in case Darko happened to glance out the window. They took a cement staircase up to the second floor, bypassed a pool of something Emma didn't want to consider, and moved down to unit 215.

Colton gave her a quick glance. "Shelly Kern."

Emma rubbed his arm. "Whatever you say, Ricky."

Colton stumbled for words and ended up grinning. Emma had a hard time telling if he was amused or annoyed by her flagrant display of attraction, but either way, his attitude was working. She could feel their energies jousting. And if that was the case, so would Jack Darko, if the man had any sense whatsoever.

He took a deep breath and knocked on the door. "Feel free to keep channeling this...tension. Whatever you're doing...."

Emma didn't respond. It was best to keep him guessing. That would keep things electric.

Colton knocked for a second time.

If this was going to happen, she wanted it to happen *now*.

For a second, Emma didn't expect an answer, the air remained so quiet, but then footsteps sounded out inside. "You better not be trying to sell me anything, 'less it contains plenty of sugar!"

Emma pulled her lips into a pout and kept her hand on Colton's bicep.

The door jerked open, and a skinny man on the taller side in a Miami Dolphins t-shirt and jeans stood framed in the doorway. His pale, lightly freckled face opened wide into a grin, and before Emma could react, he'd stepped forward and wrapped Colton in a hug. She pulled back, just avoiding an elbow in the face.

"Man, if it isn't good to see you. How are ya? Who's the chick?"

Colton laughed, patting him on the back before he pulled away. "I'm good. And it's good to see you too. How ya been?"

"Gettin' by, gettin' by." The man stepped back and gave Emma a long up-and-down appraisal, sweeping one hand through his black hair as he did. "But again, my man, the chick?"

"The chick is Shelly Kern. You can call me Shell." Emma took possession of her man again.

Colton's smile turned a touch more serious as he looked down at Emma.

She met his eyes in return, channeling the woman from her past and how she'd look at Oren. Authenticity was crucial in an op.

Colton's face softened as he set his hand over hers. "Shell is a...good friend of mine." Releasing her, he turned back to Darko. "I'm hoping you have a minute for us."

"Sure, sure." Darko stepped back and opened the door wide. "Anything for my boy Rick. Depending on what the 'anything' is, right?" He laughed, darting a *cat that ate the canary* grin at Emma.

Colton led Emma inside. "Thanks, man. We won't take much time, and I'll make it worth your while."

Darko shut the door behind them, hard. "What've you been up to, anyway? Shit sucked, the way you got booted out of, uh..." He coughed, his gaze coming back to Emma.

Keeping her eyes wide and innocent—with a heavy measure of dingbat tossed in—she studied the room as if she'd never seen walls before.

"I've been here and there." Colton led the way into Darko's living room and turned to face him.

The space was surprisingly nice, considering the outside. A neat kitchen took up one half of the open area, and a modern-furnished living room the rest. A hallway stretched out away from them, and Emma just caught the flip of a tabby cat's tail as it sauntered into one of the rooms.

"Took a bit of a vacay down in the Carolinas to get some cash flow goin'."

"Nice, nice." Darko collapsed into an armchair, waving them toward his couch. "Things are the same here. Cash situation's not bad, but I wouldn't mind my own vacation, I gotta tell ya."

Colton laughed easily, and Emma found herself impressed by how well he could lie. Sure, she'd known he'd been undercover for a while, but he'd done such a shitty job of fitting in with the team, she hadn't expected him to appear so at ease now. When the situation called for it, he could lie with the best of them. Even his language had changed, if slightly.

"Anyhow, I'd love to catch up soon, but I have to tell ya, I'm here on business." Colton set a hand on the outside of Emma's knee, pulling her a bit closer, his voice going a little more serious. "Shell here's been dealing with a scumbag of an ex. Guy's been harassing her left and right, and she tried going to the cops, but they blew her off."

"Even after the son of a bitch hit me…" Emma made eye contact with Darko and held it, her lower lip trembling just right. She could be a victim without *playing* the victim.

Darko bowed his head and shook it. He'd bought it.

Colton gazed down at Emma with a loving expression and squeezed her knee in comfort. "He didn't leave a mark. Guy's smart. Careful when he pushed her around, but he's dangerous. And the police aren't gonna step in 'til he puts her in the hospital. It's been three months since she dumped his ass. I finally convinced her she can't wait any longer."

Darko gave a little hum of manly disgust.

They'd pushed his protective caveman button perfectly. Darko eyed her again with a sympathetic frown. "Police rarely help when someone actually needs it. No surprise there. Don't take it personally, Shell."

She nodded, adding the tiniest of smiles.

Colton let go of Emma's knee and leaned forward, resting his elbows on his thighs. "This dude is *relentless*, Jack. He showed up at our gym this mornin'. Seven in the fuckin' morning. Walked in with some of his crew. Me and a few of the guys chased him off, but Shell tells me he's been waitin' for her outside her work too, and more'n once, and it's happenin' more often and at different places."

Darko leaned back in his armchair, crossing one leg over

the other. "You talking about Frank's gym that we used to go to? Surprised Frank ain't already shot the bastard."

Colton laughed. "That'd make it easier. But Frank closed his place. Found out right when I got back into town. Jack... you wouldn't be—"

"Testing you?" Darko grinned, back to the good ole boy act. "Gotta be on my toes, right? But, yeah, that shit's a shame. I go to a place over on Eighth now."

Colton nodded. "Thing is, we can take care of the gym, but we aren't a fuckin' security detail. The dude's relentless, so we need something ASAP. No time to wait on a permit, ya know? That'd be more than a week. Plus, if Shell has to use it..."

"Better not to have it traced back to her, I got ya." Darko nodded without hesitation. "Just in case."

Emma gripped tighter to Colton's arm to keep him from responding right away. This was the time when she *needed* to say something. She licked her lips, pushing a subtle undertone of nerves into her voice. "I'm not afraid to defend myself, but he's more than twice my size, and there are usually two or three of them. I never should've let it go this far." She shook her head in disgust just to drive it home.

"Hey, some guys are just born pricks. This ain't your fault, Shell."

"Thank you, Jack, I appreciate that. Rick just convinced me this morning to get 'proactive,' if you know what I mean. I've never owned a gun, but I've shot one, you know, as a kid out in the woods." She looked at Colton. "When Rick said he might know someone who could help..."

Darko was nodding. "No worries, girl, you came to the right place. I think I can find you something." His focus went back to Colton, and a sly grin crossed his lips. "We been uppin' our game lately, man, in every way, in case you're in the market for other shit."

Colton leaned forward. "Every way? Don't tell me you've started smokin' that shit crystal clear that Marty used to light up with."

"Hell, no. That shit ain't been on the street for months, man. Dried up and blew off in the wind or somethin'. Nah, I'm serious, though. You need anything else, I'm your guy."

Colton nodded and reached sideways to wrap Emma into a side-armed hug.

She leaned in, placing a hand on the inside of his leg.

"Cost's no problem, Jack. I'm flush from a few jobs, and Shell's salt of the earth. I got her covered. Whatever it takes."

"You got it on ya?"

Colton pulled a thick envelope that'd been tucked into the back of his sweatpants. "That enough?"

Darko flipped through the envelope, counting silently. With a grin, he nodded and stood, shaking Colton's hand and pulling him to his feet.

Colton pulled Emma up with him, and Jack ushered them to the door. "Gimme a little time to make the calls, and we'll get you all set up."

"Thanks, man." Colton clapped a hand on the other man's shoulder.

Darko tugged him into a bro hug. "Damn, it's good to see you." He pulled back. "And nice to meet you, Shell."

"You, too, Jack. Thank you. I mean it."

Darko stared at her a minute before turning to Colton with a laugh. "Damn, you've got a type." He turned and closed the door.

Colton and Emma kept up the charade, walking hand in hand until they were down the hall and around the corner.

He stopped at the staircase and turned to her, mouth slightly open.

She cocked her head, keeping a neutral look plastered on

in case anyone was watching from the shadows. "What? Spit it out."

"That's not how I pictured that going down, but it felt good. It felt—"

"Real." She answered for him. It had felt real. They made a good team, even if he was irritating as all shit.

"Yeah. It was like we were partners. How'd you know to play him like that? I was thinking victim."

"Boring. Anyway, a guy like Rick Dwyer would need to be invested to want to help. So I played the 'good friend.'"

"A very good friend." Colton looked away, and Emma wondered if he was fighting off the urge to blush.

"Just doing my job. And it's no wonder you got put on undercover. I'm impressed. And that money?"

"I've still got an undercover budget, so it's just a matter of paperwork. Figured we might need it." The grin became more honest.

"Hey, what did he mean by 'you've got a type?'"

"I dunno. Attractive women, maybe." Colton turned and led the way down the stairs.

"Hey, did you notice he fits the profile?"

"I've got eyes."

"But you already knew him, so you already knew that. Something you wanna tell me, Colton? You think Darko might be worth looking into?"

Colton shot her a glance over his shoulder and shrugged.

So Jack Darko fit the profile. But was he selling guns stolen from the Salem PD armory? And was he also using them to kill cops?

*You'll get to the truth, Emma girl, especially now that you've got this weapons deal going.*

## 30

At the park across the street, Emma pulled out her phone and dialed Jacinda as soon as they got back to the car. In a shaded spot beneath some trees, they practically blended into the shadows.

"How'd it go?" Jacinda spoke fast, her voice through the speaker betraying just how much she was hoping for the best.

Emma smiled. She was excited they'd made such headway.

"Perfectly." Mia answered for her. "They both deserve Oscars."

"We're parked across from Darko's complex." Emma eyed it. "There's only one exit since the place is surrounded by a poor excuse for a gate, and we'll see him if he leaves. Darko said he can get us a gun, probably today."

Colton leaned toward the phone. "Jacinda, Darko and I are on good terms, but if the plan's still to tail whoever drops off the weapon to him, we ought to change me out with someone else, since I could be recognized. Nobody but Darko's seen Emma, so she'll be good to go."

"I'll send Leo to take your place." Jacinda conferred with someone on her end and then came back on the line. "Send me the location, and I'll get Leo out there ASAP."

Counting her breaths, centering herself yet again, Emma signed off the call with Jacinda.

Colton's phone dinged within seconds of Emma tucking her phone away, and she glanced over to see him reading a text.

"This must be Darko's new number, which might come in handy. He said he's got the hookup, so we're good to go. He just needs a few hours. Says he'll have it by one."

"And the good news keeps on coming." Emma settled back in her seat.

Colton offered her gum, and the three of them sat back to wait.

Barely an hour had passed before Leo pulled into the spot next to where they'd parked. Emma offered Colton a nod of thanks and gave Mia a quick smile before she ducked out of the car. Seconds later, Colton pulled out and disappeared down the street, Mia in his passenger seat.

Mia seemed fine, Emma was relieved to note. Maybe she hadn't liked taking a back seat, but having something to focus on other than Vance had clearly done her some good. And maybe understanding she couldn't bring her relationship problems into the office did too. Though, admittedly, Emma felt bad about that. They had mostly been fighting about her.

"Thanks for coming." Emma nodded at Leo's outfit. "I'm glad you changed into jeans. No telling if we'll end up back here to pick up the gun."

He rolled the windows down and gestured to the coffees in the cup holders. "Front one's yours if you want it."

"Oh, you are a godsend." Emma picked up the cup and took a long drink. Relaxing with a decent cup of coffee was sometimes the best part of a stakeout. "So Darko fits the profile."

Leo paused mid-sip and took the cup away from his lips slowly. "You think Colton inadvertently led us to our potential killer?"

"If he did, it's no happy accident."

Leo settled back into his seat, gazing across at the apartment complex. "Seems like today went off without a hitch, though. And now we just need that gun to see where it might lead us."

Emma grimaced. "Anything new on your end of the investigation?"

He huffed a laugh. "Well, I've narrowed down FBI agents who fit the profile and whose last names are Knight. I'm down to twelve solid potential suspects. One is retired and sixty, and two are mid-fifties, which feels unlikely to me for some reason. But all of them are six feet, give or take. Blond to medium-brown hair. Thinner but fit. All white."

"That's a good place to start. What about Vance?" Emma almost didn't want to ask, after the ass chewing Jacinda had given Mia.

"Vance pulled his shit together enough to deep-dive into Darby. So far, nothing. But he's narrowing down the Knights."

It just didn't make sense that Darby was a random hit.

"Hey…I want to apologize for pushing you and everyone to think of Colton as a suspect. I shouldn't have pushed so hard."

"Not your fault." Emma wondered how long things would've gone on if she and Leo hadn't managed to follow him the night before. "Colton was acting truly suspicious, and we all knew it. Hell, when we were tailing him that close to the Eighth, I thought you were a hundred percent right."

Relief flashed across Leo's face. "I'm kind of glad I wasn't alone. I got to thinking about it this morning and felt like an ass."

Emma laughed, and they settled into an easy silence. Being with Leo, back with a familiar partner, brought along its own sense of comfort. Colton might've been a capable agent and a skilled actor, but he was new to the team. On a stakeout or a tail, Emma wanted to be at the side of someone she could trust to have her back based on personal experience, not just the badge.

They watched for Darko's car to leave, but it didn't. Within an hour, though, a maroon Honda Civic pulled into the apartment complex and took a right and then a fast left, heading toward Darko's place. It was newer than most of the cars in the lot and without any identifying decals or bumper stickers.

"Latest candidate," Emma murmured. "If he leaves soon…"

"We'll know." Leo straightened in his seat, watching. They'd already kept an eagle eye out for four other vehicles that had entered, waiting to see if any of them would go in for just long enough to drop off a weapon, then leave again. So far, all the cars that had gone into the complex had stayed there.

But this one reappeared within three minutes. Emma's phone dinged just as it came back into view, and she looked down to see a text from Colton.

*Drop-off just happened. Jack's got the gun.*

Emma showed Leo the text, and he tugged on his seat belt and started the SUV up. They pulled into traffic a few cars behind the maroon sedan, and Emma texted Jacinda they were in pursuit. She'd snapped a photo of the driver as the sedan had turned onto the street and sent that along, for what good it would do. A profile shot at a distance.

Weaving in and out of traffic to stay a few car lengths

behind, Leo kept him in sight as they trailed him all the way across the city and into a warehouse district. Down the road from where the man parked on the curb, he pulled into a storage-unit business.

Their guy hurried into a warehouse, and they got their first good look at his clothes. A white long-sleeved t-shirt featuring an unfamiliar logo stretched over his gut. His whitewashed jeans rode low on his hips while a ball cap hid most of his face. Thick black hair peeked out the back.

Emma sent the license plate number in to Jacinda, and once they had a location, Jacinda texted back. *I've got plainclothes MPD en route to your location to relieve you and keep watch. Head back to HQ when they arrive.*

Sighing, Emma pocketed the phone after showing the text to Leo. "I guess it makes sense. We could be waiting here for hours. But still."

Leo settled deep into his seat. "I know what you mean. It's too tempting to get out and take a closer look right now."

"Which is probably why Jacinda wants us back at the Bureau." Their SSA knew them way too well. "But maybe they've got something new."

*Or maybe this guy'll come out and be on the move before MPD arrives, and we'll stay with him.*

A woman could only hope.

## 31

Back at the Bureau, Emma separated from Leo and slipped into the locker room, where she changed out of her black fitted thermal and jeans and back into her slacks, blouse, and jacket.

When she got to her desk, Leo was waiting for her, and they headed into Jacinda's office together. She waved them to take seats.

"Colton and Mia are finishing up their reports while Vance narrows down the Knights. Colton's already confirmed that he's not familiar with the warehouse where our delivery driver ended up. I have a request for a warrant in already, so we'll see how fast that happens." Jacinda glanced back and forth between them. "Anything else to report?"

"Nothing you don't already know." Emma shifted in her chair. She wanted the next steps to be happening *now*. "Where do you want us?"

"You and Leo look into the owner of the car." Jacinda passed a printout of a DMV file across her desk. "His name is Norman Little...and get this. There are *six* different vehicles registered to him. One of them is an old Toyota RAV4, green. And his address goes to a shitty apartment. Facts aren't adding up."

Leo leaned over to take a glance at Little's picture. "That's not the guy who was driving our car."

Jacinda raised an eyebrow. "You're sure? I thought you didn't get a good look."

Emma nodded agreement. "That's true, but our driver today had a belly on him, and he was short. Dark hair. Based on height and weight alone, this isn't the same guy."

Narrowing her eyes, Jacinda bit her lip for a second before nodding. "All right, well, that makes this guy even more interesting. Plus—"

"Little fits the profile." Emma finished her sentence. *How many times am I going to say that sentence in one day?* "Just like Jack Darko."

"Suspects are just falling from the sky today." Leo held his hands out, like he was expecting yet another one to descend from the ceiling.

"Dig into both of them and see what you find. We need to know if he's a fake or not, and we need to know fast. Or if maybe someone's just using him as a cover to own a bunch of cars used by a criminal enterprise."

A second later, Emma settled back at her desk, typing away as Jacinda headed to her office. "I'll take Little." The first search proved the man was indeed real and not in any apparent position to own six cars. "He's coming up as a known affiliate of his father, Barry Little, who worked with the Cloaks."

Leo grunted. "Makes sense, given he dropped off a gun at Darko's. Speaking of, he doesn't even have a record."

"No record, huh? Interesting." She turned her attention back to her screen. "Looks like this Barry Little was moving drugs heavily until a year ago, when he got caught in a pretty big drug bust. Little's in jail."

"Could be why our guy has it out for law enforcement. If Norman Little's our guy." Leo cracked his neck in a series of impressive pops. "Nothing else comes up on him?"

Shaking her head, Emma gave up on government records and typed his name into a web search. "Nothing but the DMV records. He's twenty-four, and there's no known employer listed, but that may or may not mean anything, depending on what he's doing for money. His apartment's not far. Shall we?"

Leo grinned, already pulling on his jacket. "No way to know he's our guy if we don't talk to him."

"And for whatever reason, Jack Darko doesn't feel like our guy, even though he's not clean. He's just a criminal without a record." Emma glanced toward the conference room, where Mia and Vance were at separate ends of the table and typing away at their laptops.

"That's diplomatic." But Leo was already nodding as he headed toward Jacinda's office. "Let's run it by Jacinda. If she agrees, we can go talk to this Norman Little while Mia and Vance run his picture by our witnesses and see if we've got pay dirt. He's certainly got the build of the guy in the garage video."

At his knock, Jacinda glanced up from her computer. "Find anything?"

"What little there is, pun intended." Emma adjusted her bag on her shoulder. "I think we've got enough to head to Little's apartment and question him. He's real. Comes up in records as a known affiliate of his father, who's sitting in federal prison. Was a drug runner for the Cloaks. Which means we have our motive that sets him up to hate law enforcement."

"We're thinking we split up." Leo gestured over his

shoulder, toward the conference room. "Emma and I can see if knocking on his door gets him to come out. Meanwhile, Mia and Vance can run his picture by our witnesses and see if we get anywhere."

Jacinda's lip quirked. "I appreciate you two thinking like that. Colton's upstairs filing a report with his higher-ups. After that, he's going to get the gun from Darko. He'll be fine without you, Emma. It's an established relationship. And then he'll bring that to ballistics." She paused and assessed them.

Emma wasn't sure what the boss was thinking.

"But we're going to split you up differently."

Leo and Emma exchanged a glance.

"Emma, you take Vance for the knocking on doors. Leo, you and Mia run the picture by witnesses."

Emma almost protested, but she could count on one hand the times Jacinda had changed her mind once an order came out. She knew Jacinda was trying to get her team to function as a cohesive unit again, and Emma didn't envy her that task.

Maybe this was Emma's chance to convince Vance that he didn't need to worry about working with her. And she knew she could work with him.

Jacinda waved them out. "So you four get going."

Hurrying back out of Jacinda's office, Emma speed-walked toward the conference room with Leo on her heels. Whether Norman Little was their unsub or not, he was a solid lead, and she was ready to follow it.

## 32

Leo pulled to a stop a few blocks from their destination, waiting for yet another red light to turn green. Traffic wasn't bad, but he'd hit nearly every light so far. He sighed and stretched in the seat.

"Neither one of us is having a good day, huh?" Mia tucked some hair behind her ears, the barest hint of a smile on her lips. "You've seemed anxious."

"Guilty, more like." The light turned green, and Leo hit the gas a touch harder than intended. "After pushing so hard yesterday for us to take a real look at Colton, I feel like I wasted everyone's time. But it's good to be doing something. You okay?"

Mia shrugged. "You may as well know now. I broke it off with Vance after Colton and I came back to the Bureau."

Leo shot her a quick glance, wishing he wasn't driving so he could study her features. Not that the admission was of particular surprise, the way their relationship was spiraling, but he wouldn't have expected the breakup to happen at the office or for her to be the one to tell him. "Shit. I'm sorry, Mia."

"It was bound to happen sooner than later." Mia pointed ahead to the left, but he'd already seen the bail bond sign coming up. "I'd never blame it on Emma, but since she revealed her ability to him and Jacinda, it's like every bit of trust between us has dissipated. I thought it was starting to get better, but it didn't last. He always thinks people are hiding something from him."

Leo pulled into the business's small parking lot, searching for the right words. "I didn't help yesterday since we both thought Colton was hiding even more than he was. That might've fed into Vance's paranoia too. He just needs more time. It wasn't easy for me to accept Emma's confession about the Other, no matter how I acted. Inside my head, the wheels were turning constantly…I just maybe put on a better front of believing her at first, compared to Vance. Hell, it's still hard for me to believe in Emma's ability, but I do."

"Maybe." Mia unbuckled her seat belt, visibly refocusing on the case. "But I won't hold my breath."

Leo shifted in his seat, trying to keep his mind on the present. He'd had such good reason to believe Emma, but he wouldn't wish that on Vance or anyone else.

Hearing Emma tell him that she was seeing Denae's ghost, giving him what they'd both thought would be her last message and words to him…he'd felt like he was dying too. Being sucked into a cyclone of despair and anger and confusion. And this was even after Denae had pulled through and confirmed what she'd seen—that she'd talked to him through Emma…

Leo still had trouble believing in Emma's Other. Well, at least understanding it. He'd gotten there, but it hadn't been easy. Nothing seemed easy anymore, though.

More thankful than ever to be out of traffic, Leo hurried to the business's door and pulled it open. A citrusy scent drifted out, and they stepped inside to find a portly man sitting behind a desk with a stack of paperwork in front of him. Incense drifted up from one corner.

His attention focused immediately on Mia. "You again. Didn't get enough of me before? Needed to come back with a new partner?"

Leo adopted a friendly smile and stepped up to the desk, flashing his credentials. "Special Agent Leo Ambrose. And you're Louis Robinson?"

"I am." The man dropped his black pen on top of the paperwork and stared at them.

"I was afraid we wouldn't find you here." Mia slipped into one of the hard chairs before his desk, and Leo sat beside her. "With you preferring to work nights and all."

Robinson huffed. "My daytime guy had a dentist appointment this afternoon, so I guess it's your lucky day. Let me guess, you want me to tell the whole story you already heard from the beginning? Or no, you want me to tell it twice?"

The man pressed some of his frizzy hair down, frowning, but Leo shook his head.

"We have new evidence. This'll just take a minute." Leo pulled up Norman Little's photo on his phone, courtesy of the DMV, and held it in front of Louis Robinson. "Does this look like the man you saw in an FBI jacket Monday morning?"

His eyes narrowed, and he scratched one finger against the side of his lip as he considered the photo. "Like I told Agent Logan and her other partner, I didn't get a look at the guy's face. But based on this photo and the guy's info, I'd guess they have about the same height and build. And this guy's hair is short. Mr. FBI Getup had his hair covered by a hat, but this is consistent with what I did see. And it was on the blonder side too. Like this guy."

Mia leaned forward. "And have you ever seen this man before?"

Robinson's lips turned downward into a deep frown, and he shook his head. "I've got an eye for faces when I've got enough light to see 'em by. This guy's a complete stranger to me."

Leo stood up as he tucked his phone away. "Thanks for your time, Mr. Robinson. We appreciate it."

Outside, Leo led the way back to the SUV. Linda Weller was their next stop.

He remembered the way to their last crime scene well enough that he didn't need to worry about inputting the address. "Robinson just the same as you saw him before? No alarm bells?"

Mia chuckled. "If anything, he was calmer. When Emma and I met him Monday, he picked up that little incense carrier and took a big, direct whiff of the smoke. I'd never seen anything like it."

"That's one way to get high, I guess." Leo relaxed into his seat as he cruised through a yellow light in a way that would've made Emma happy. "But let's hope our other witness can give us more."

Linda Weller's house appeared the same as before, charming as could be minus the damaged bed of colorful tulips that she'd attempted to nurse back to life after falling on top of them. Across the street from her home, their crime scene looked like any other nice suburban house.

Leo only gave the barest of glances to where they'd found Officer Gorik's body. No trace of the man, and Emma wasn't there to tell him if his ghost was hanging around.

The brick walkway to Linda Weller's house bypassed the crushed tulips and some pretty lavender flowers that he was sure Yaya would've been able to put a name to. He nodded at the hose coiled behind some shrubs against the house. "No wonder she leaves it out. This garden must take a lot of time."

"Lucky for us." Mia rapped on the window in the door. "Unlucky for Gorik. I bet our killer watched her daily. I bet she's the connection. He clearly wanted a witness, and I bet he found one in our little horticulturist."

"That's an interesting point. We certainly can't find a connection to Martha Lancaster's house, so that might be it."

"Coming!" The woman's voice filtered through the door. Seconds later, the same curly gray hair could be seen through the window in the door as locks clicked. Linda opened it up with a smile that dimmed noticeably as soon as she saw them. "Hello."

Leo offered the friendliest, calmest smile he had. "How are you, Mrs. Weller? I trust you got to see your doctor?"

She nodded, brushing her hands off on a *Kiss the Cook* apron scattered with flowers. "I did. Man says there's not a thing wrong with me or my mind. I'm debating getting a second opinion. Maybe something you two tell me will help me decide. Do you want to come in?"

Mia shook her head, her phone already in hand. "No, ma'am, we won't trouble you for that. We just want you to take a look at a photo, if you could."

"My biscuits are in the oven. It's fine." The woman leaned in toward Mia's phone as she held it up and then touched it gently to reposition Mia's hand and allow herself to see it better. "Am I supposed to know him?"

Leo's hopes flagged. The woman before them wanted to help but only looked confused. "We were hoping you might recognize him. He's not familiar?"

Linda's nose wrinkled as she bent closer to the phone. "I didn't get a good look at your killer, and I imagine that's who you're asking me about. I saw his profile, remember, and based on this DMV shot...I just don't know. It could be him, but this man could also be anyone. I can't tell you, but he's not familiar to me."

*Profile, right.*

Leo pulled out his own phone and offered her the profile shot Emma had gotten of their delivery driver. This time, though, the woman only shook her head. "I won't say that's him, no. Seems too…big-like. The dark hair. Nope. But I'm sorry I can't be of more help."

Tucking away his phone, Leo thanked her for her time, with Mia echoing the sentiment. They'd go to the other witness's house next, Elizabeth Soyinka, but considering she hadn't even remembered seeing an agent, he didn't hold out hope for a positive ID. As the two of them made their way back down the flower-lined walkway, he steeled himself for another useless interview.

He sure hoped Emma and Vance were getting somewhere faster.

## 33

Emma glanced sideways at Vance, who'd been scowling into the distance throughout their drive. The windshield might as well have been his mortal enemy.

Truly, she had no desire to bring up his relationship with Mia…but she had even less desire to watch his attitude deteriorate further. If Norman Little or some witness rubbed him wrong, and he was as tense as a live wire, she could imagine plenty of nightmare scenarios.

*Especially considering the way he flipped out on that street artist when Mia'd been kidnapped. Those emotions are the same ones that made him run straight into a warehouse explosion.*

Emma cringed at the memory, even more so because she'd understood his high-octane behavior. How many lectures or too-meaningful glances had she gotten, telling her she'd run off on her own again one time too many? Well, no, *many times* too many.

Which meant, for both her sake and Vance's, this wasn't a time to let him stew in his own emotions until they exploded all over the case.

"Vance, I'm sorry to ask, but it's clear you're not just

thinking about the case. And I couldn't help noticing how silent you and Mia were in the conference room." She paused, waiting for him to take the lead, and continued only when he didn't. "Is everything okay between you?"

His lips thinned, and for a moment, she thought he'd ignore her. Then…

"We broke up this morning. Or, rather, she broke up with me."

*Shit. I should've known.*

Emma took a deep breath, pressing on the gas pedal to get them to Little's just a touch faster. "If you…want to talk about it, we—"

"I don't." His clipped answer hung in the air, and he turned his face to the side window, avoiding her gaze entirely.

Emma wished she hadn't asked. This wasn't exactly an improvement over silence. "Are the two of you going to be okay working the case together? And at the office? You can't exactly avoid each other, and I know…"

She didn't know what she'd been about to say, actually. She was just blathering on like Mrs. Kellerly as she drifted through her door while Emma drank her morning coffee.

But Vance twisted toward her, fire in his gaze. "Maybe you should go ask a ghost, Emma. They seem to know everything."

She slowed the vehicle, thankful they weren't dealing with much traffic. Taking a deep breath, she fought down annoyance. Meeting his animosity with her own wouldn't help. "You want to tell me where that came from?"

"I'm sick of you having all the answers, that's where." He shifted in his seat, adjusting his jacket and wiping off some nonexistent fuzz. "Do you know how frustrating it is to work hard to solve a case, only to have you swoop in with your little ghosts and the right answers every time? What's the point of me even being on the case?"

"Ghosts aren't solving this case for us."

"Really? I beg to differ. I've been neck-deep in FBI agents with the last name Knight for the last two hours!"

"Knight didn't just come from a ghost, but from Linda Weller. She heard the agent. And, besides, you're the one that put what the ghost said together, Vance. You're the one that said night meant Knight with a *K*!"

*Calm down, Emma girl. He's trying to get under your skin.*

And he was doing a fine job of it too.

"Don't patronize me."

Emma hardened her voice. "I don't have to take your abuse. You're acting like a pouting toddler who wants all the attention. If I really had all the answers, like you claim, why would I have confronted Colton with Leo? Why would anyone have needed to go undercover with him? Hmm? And why would I have gotten Norman Little's name, with Jacinda and Leo, by the way, from DMV records instead of one of my *little ghosts*, as you so eloquently put it?"

He huffed. "Woe is Emma that she had to do work."

A "screw you" almost came off Emma's tongue for the second time today, but she bit it down. "I know you're pissed. Mia broke up with you, and you and Leo were barking up the wrong tree when you were so sure an FBI agent in our midst was killing cops. Your pride's wounded, but fuck if I'll let you talk to me like that. Ghosts haven't been any help on this case, and you know it, so grow up already. Or if you're not up to doing the job without letting your emotions control you, call Jacinda and tell her yourself."

Vance breathed deep, and she heard him counting to five under his breath. She tried to do the same, but found she couldn't keep quiet.

Emma did soften her voice just a touch, though. Carrots

instead of sticks and all that. "I'm sorry, Vance, but you're either up to being my partner today or not. Yeah, I was skeptical of your and Leo's theory, and I went against it, but that had nothing to do with ghosts. I'm a good agent, with or without the help of anything else. You knew me and my work before I ever had access to the Other, remember? And you respected me then."

It took several seconds before he nodded. "You always had my back. But while everyone seems to follow you, what respect do I get in return? Maybe that's part of the issue here, Emma. That I get a drip-feed of respect like I'm a tagalong puppy, like my work is nonexistent, and it's just assumed I'll do my job, keep quiet, and go home. Well, finally, I've spoken up because the status quo has gotten old."

Emma's breath left her, heavy and uncomfortable. Was that really how he'd felt through all these months working together? She stared out the windshield, focusing on the street as her head swam. "I thought we were a team. I…still do. I never knew you felt like that."

He remained quiet another moment before continuing. "I didn't used to. But things change."

*Ain't that the truth.*

"Yeah, but some things don't." She took a deep breath, forcing her voice to remain calm. "I solve cases by considering every angle and investigating situations thoroughly before drawing conclusions. Normally, that's *all* of us. Period. And I respect you, just like I respect the rest of the team."

He snorted. "Sure."

She ignored the sarcasm. "I can't say why you and Leo got tunnel vision on your theory about Colton. But it's over now. And we need to move forward. We've finally got a solid lead. As a team, leaving emotions out of it. So again, are you up to it? Because if you're not, I'll damn well pull over, and you can call a fucking Uber for all I care."

Vance stretched his hands in his lap, and for a moment, Emma thought he might punch her or the dash instead of answering. After another long exhale, he nodded. "You're right that my emotions are getting the best of me currently."

He sounded like a robot, but she kept her mouth shut.

"I apologize for that much. And I take your point. You were a good agent…before. I know you still are."

She bristled, but bit down on her lip, trying to remember what it felt like to have a promising and loving relationship go up in smoke. The powerlessness of it, even aside from the rest of what they were dealing with.

When he remained silent, she said what she had to. "Look, Vance, I know breakups are hard. I get it. But, please, don't take your emotions out on me. I don't deserve that, full stop."

Vance's lip quirked, disdain radiating from his expression. "Isn't that a bit like the pot calling the kettle black? You've stepped on toes and pushed into interviews where you were told to take a back seat, and we've all dealt with the repercussions. I'm not the only piece of work sitting in this car."

Emma's cheeks heated, but she couldn't disagree. Eventually, she offered a weak, half-sincere smile. "Well then, from one piece of work to another, how about we try to do better?"

He slouched in his seat, blinking hard, and she realized her softer tone had probably, finally, won the day enough to allow them to work. "I agree. And…I am sorry."

*Less of the robot, more of the Vance I know. Thank goodness.*

"I'm sorry too." She meant it.

"I've been so angry lately, and the emotions have been hard to control, but I'll do better. And as you said, it's not fair for me to take it out on you. But I promise you I'm up to the case, so I'd appreciate it if we could just forget this conversation happened and go find Little. If it's all the same to you." He kept his gaze on the window, but his voice had become calmer.

That had to be a good sign.

Emma breathed deep, channeling Oren's words and forcing some of the tension out of her shoulders. If she hadn't worried about him interrogating her every action, she might've gripped the little crystal in her pocket, too, but this was definitely not the time for that.

She nodded again, partly to herself. "Okay, good. Let's do this."

The rest of the drive passed quickly, and the GPS led them to an apartment complex that looked like a thousand others in D.C. A tall cement building painted a slate gray. And with a gazillion windows, it could've passed for a government building, though the landscaping, swimming pool, and dog park spread on the outskirts of the large parking lot proved it to be residential.

Parking, she glanced again at Norman Little's address, then looked up at the building. "Not fancy, but not dismal. Definitely not something Little could afford if he's unemployed."

"Agreed." Vance climbed from the SUV, Emma right behind him. "Which means he's working under the table. Doesn't exactly sound like the trust fund type, given that his father's in prison."

Emma adjusted her bag on her shoulder and led the way toward the front entrance.

A woman walking out with her poodle on a leash held the door for them with a smile, and Emma returned it easily. Waiting at the elevator, she glanced around to make sure nobody was looking before addressing Vance. "Not a suspicious place. Norman Little can't be the norm here if his dad was gang-affiliated like the records show."

"How long has he lived here?" Vance stepped into the elevator as it arrived.

Emma pulled up his DMV information on her phone. "His license was just reissued five months ago, and he lived here then. That doesn't mean he's lived here for all that long, though."

On the fifth floor, they moved into a wide carpeted hallway, where fluorescents ran the length of the ceiling. It looked like an office building.

"Not as pleasant as the downstairs amenities would suggest." Vance raised his eyebrow at a door festooned with entrepreneurial advertisements for makeup. "But I guess that makes it more affordable."

They stopped at unit 527. Nothing decorated this door except the garden-variety peephole, and when Emma knocked, they got no response. Vance tried next, and Emma fought to hear any sound that might signal Little was inside avoiding them. But everything was silent.

"Shall we knock on some doors?"

Nodding, Vance moved up to the next door over, knocked, and got no answer. Emma took the next one and, again, got no response.

At the fifth door they tried, though, an older woman opened up. Her thin brown hair was pulled up in a bun, and Emma judged her to be in her sixties. Offering her best smile, she pulled out her credentials. The woman adjusted her glasses and leaned close, then nodded.

Emma made the introductions and asked for a few minutes of her time.

"All right. I'm Amy Calvino. I'm sure it's nice to meet you…" She frowned, one hand fidgeting with the buttons of her sweater. "Or it will be until you tell me why the FBI's knocking on my door. This isn't about my daughter, is it? She swore to me she paid those parking tickets…"

"It's not, Mrs. Calvino." Vance had his customary charm about him again, and Emma was grateful to see it. "I'm sure she did pay the tickets. We'd just like to ask if you happen to know this man."

He held his phone up for the woman's viewing, and she squinted at it, readjusting her glasses before nodding. "That's Norman, all right. Last name Little. Lived here a couple of years and comes and goes at all hours. Is he in trouble?"

Emma offered a noncommittal smile. "That's what we're trying to find out. What can you tell us about him? You said he comes and goes at odd hours?"

Mrs. Calvino pursed her lips and leaned on her doorframe, clutching her sweater closer. "A bit. I go out every day to walk my Guinness…my beagle, I mean…and I've seen him coming in around the time. Saw him talking to some nefarious-looking characters one time, too, though I guess that was a while ago. I think some snow was on the ground, if I remember right."

"You've never overheard any of his conversations?" Vance flashed his best open expression, eyes bright. "It could really help us out."

"Well…" She hesitated, glancing down the hall as if to ensure Little wouldn't show up and hear her. "I did hear him having a shouting match with a man who I would've taken for one of the city's homeless. It was a while ago. He was saying something about the city going downhill. I just took it for an angry temper and have kept my distance. I fear that's all I can tell you, though."

Emma handed over her card. "If you remember anything that might be helpful, no matter how small, please, call. And if you happen to see Mr. Little come back, I'd appreciate a call then too."

The woman nodded, and Emma had a feeling she was the type who would sit by the window for hours, just for the thrill of being involved.

At the next door, she was just about to give up on getting another answer to her knock when a middle-aged man came to his door, rubbing his eyes. He gazed blearily at their IDs. "FBI, huh? This have something to do with the young guy down the hall?"

*Bingo.*

Emma had her phone in front of her a second later. "Do you mean this man?"

The man narrowed his eyes on her, rolling his shoulders back as if he'd just woken up. Judging by his messy hair, she guessed he might have. But he looked back at the picture and nodded.

Emma pressed on. "What can you tell us about him?"

A flash of disgust crossed his features. "I can tell you that I don't like the way he looks, how he's skulking all the time."

"Skulking?" Vance managed to keep his question level, despite the use of the atypical word choice.

The man glanced from side to side. "He's always looking this way and that. Lurking. Shuffling his feet like he's moving fast but without making a lot of noise. You know the type."

They did.

"Have you ever talked to him?"

"I just moved in here a few months ago, getting closer to work. I know a few names based on seeing some friendly faces on the elevator, but that's it. Not this guy so much."

"How did you know who we were going to ask about?"

"Because of what I just told you. Oh, and some woman was here, crying and yelling at him, and I heard her mention the police."

"Really?" Vance leaned against the wall, notebook out. "I don't suppose you know why?"

"Ha. Hell no. I asked, though, just this morning. People get curious. He gave me some line about his brother-in-law being gunned down while on duty. Young cop. Said the woman was his sister. But I don't buy it. She was probably a girlfriend, and he's probably wanted by the cops for grand theft auto. I've seen him drive at least four different automobiles since moving in."

Emma and Vance exchanged a quick look.

"Can you tell us your name and where you work, sir?" Emma smiled, softening the request. "Just so we can find you if we need to."

He raised a brow but shrugged. "I'm Dean Loomer, the nighttime manager for the grocery store over on Fifth. Malerman's Groceries."

Vance jotted down the name as Emma nodded her thanks. "We appreciate your time, Mr. Loomer." She handed over her card, and Vance did the same. "If you think of anything else or notice Little return, we'd also appreciate a call."

He nodded, yawning. "Gimme a few more hours of sleep, I might. I'll call you if I do."

With the door shut, Emma met Vance's eyes. "I'd say it's time to update the others and do a different kind of search on Greg Darby."

"Yeah, into his family tree." Vance shook his head. "Can you imagine if Norman Little is the brother of his wife?"

"There's our link if he is."

"And if Darby knew his brother-in-law was dirty and tried to look into it on his own…"

"It's possible that someone in the Cloaks, posing as an agent named Knight, took him down."

"That would make my afternoon of reading up on every Knight ever to become an FBI agent a total bust. Figures." Vance shook his head.

"Hey, Knight has got to mean something. Our unsub used the name for a reason. How many agents do you have left to look into?"

"Two. Everyone else has alibis for both deaths, and most of them live nowhere near here, no affiliation to us or Salem. I just haven't had time to dig into Gavin Knight, a newb at HQ in Boston, and Ron Knight, retired with honors from Connecticut. New England area."

"I can help you with that later."

Vance ignored her offer. "You send the text to Jacinda, and I'll call MPD and get some uniforms out here to sit on his place in case Little shows up again. I'm sure they'll love how many cars they get to look out for. Man, you think this guy killed his sister's husband?"

"I think there's a chance he's involved. He can't have killed Darby, though, because the officer would've recognized his brother-in-law posing as an FBI agent." She headed for the elevator. "Hey, Jessup, cheer up. We're making headway with exactly zero help from ghosts."

"Don't push it, Last."

Emma chuckled, texting Jacinda as they waited for the elevator. Things were finally going their way.

## 34

The candy in the drugstore aisle was all speaking to me. I normally ate way healthy, but this was just a guilty pleasure, minus the guilt. I finally went for the red licorice. That, and some gummy bears.

This sugar in my basket was the sort of candy my dad always gave me as a reward, but really, it was because I was missing my mother, and he didn't know how to manage that. It was amazing I didn't turn out to be three hundred pounds.

At the front counter, a middle-aged woman grinned at me. "Sweet tooth, hmm? You know, I'm pretty sweet too…"

I gave her my most dazzling smile, and she got a little lost in it.

"Just the candy." I pushed my goods a little closer to her with a quick wink.

"Oh, pardon me. You're just such a handsome young man."

"Thank you. That's very kind, ma'am."

My phone buzzed when I was halfway across the parking lot, and I hit the green icon with a grin. "What's the word, hummingbird?"

"I'm calling to tell you that your *girlfriend's* on a stakeout at Little's."

"Lydia…"

"Oh, no cutesy little monikers since you played boyfriend with Emma?"

"That was an op. I'm good at my job. I thought you noticed."

"Jack said she was all over you, that you were playing into every minute of it! Then the little prick had the gall to say he could tell we were sisters. 'Same vibe!' he said. What the fuck does Darko know about vibes?"

"You need to calm down. That was an op. And I had to be all in. I'm on enemy ground here. Eyes are everywhere. I fit in right now. They trust me. Just like we planned. This is all coming together."

"Is it?"

"Yes." I hopped into my Acura and put her on speaker. "And I have the gun from Darko. Jacinda sent me to get it, as you know. And as we've discussed, it's a gun from the Salem PD loot. So when ballistics works that out, it'll ruffle your sister's feathers to no end."

"My fucking sister is sitting outside Little's with your doppelgänger! Her feathers seem fine."

Vance Jessup. We did resemble each other loosely. Even when I was pissed off as all hell at Lydia, she still made me laugh. "Good. It'll keep 'em busy. And so will the warehouse."

"They obviously know Little's name, which means they know about all his vehicles, which means they might've seen one of them at one of the scenes."

"Yeah, they did, at Gorik's. The younger neighbor saw the make and model. It's not enough. Even if it were, they'd bring in Little, but he's not going to spill."

"How do you know?"

"Because the Cloaks'll neuter him if he does. And you'll

do even worse. Besides, he's got a massive hard-on for you, so he'll never squeak. And Emma and Company'll think they got their guy, but they don't. They'll be distracted every which way but right, and our plan moves forward with not so much as a speed bump."

Lydia let out a big, long sigh. We were on track just fine. She just needed reminding. But she had a jealous streak like I'd never seen, and I could picture her in my head still turning twenty shades of green.

"Baby girl, I am not attracted to Emma Last. I've only ever had eyes for you. You know this," I deepened my voice a couple registers, "and I'll prove it to you later."

"You think pillow talk is going to make this all better? What do you mistake me for, that dumb Kappa Kappa Gamma you met our first year at Yale?"

I wasn't referring to our bedroom antics, but I liked the way her mind worked. I tore into the bag of licorice and took out two vines. "You know you're the smartest woman I know."

She cleared her throat hard.

"The smartest person I know. Everything I do is for you, even letting Miss Emma Last hang on my arm. That was for you."

"The FBI's going to be onto you. Matter of time."

"Are you...worried? Aw, I love that." I bit into the licorice.

She muttered a curse on her end. "You'd better be right. I'm tired of wasting my time on useless assassins."

"Barnaby was a one-off. A loose cannon. Little will be fine. And Darko is solid, except for his big mouth. And I'm, well...me." I relaxed into the driver's seat, finishing off those vines and grabbing two more before starting the car. She knew I was right. Be nice to hear her say it, though.

She hung up on me.

Damn, but she could always make me laugh. I'd make her

pay for that later, and she knew it. This energy, this chemistry we'd always had between us, really kept the flame alive.

At first, yeah, we bonded over dead parents. Well, my dead mom and her absent father, who'd never been in her life. She didn't share his last name. Never even got to have a single conversation with the guy before he died. He'd wanted nothing to do with her. And her mother, who was probably getting paid by the hour in Hell right now, shipped her off as soon as she could walk, blackmailing Daddy all the while.

*Women. Do not get on their bad side.*

I couldn't believe she thought I was flirting with Emma. She knew me better than that. Lydia knew what was at stake for me. Knew how long I've wanted this too. Knew how devoted I was to getting revenge. I'd planned my whole world around it. And, hell, she was plucking members from the Cloaks to do her bidding. I did that. Me.

*What the hell, Lydia? Give a guy some credit.*

And she knew more than anything that fate had brought us together. And nothing was going to rip us apart. Certainly not some skinny bitch who killed my baby girl's mother or her team of misfits.

## 35

By the time Emma and Vance had determined that none of Norman Little's six vehicles were parked in the vicinity of the apartment building, the MPD finally showed up in an unmarked car. Emma ran them through case updates and made sure they had Little's photo as well as *all* his cars' license plates. She imagined he might only be driving one of them regularly, but they couldn't be sure which.

Walking back over to their own vehicle, she glanced at Vance. "You want to head back to HQ or get some dinner first?"

Her phone rang before he could answer, Jacinda's name flashing on the screen.

Emma put it on speaker and held it up between them. "Jacinda, you're on with me and Vance."

"Good. The gun Colton bought off Jack Darko came back stolen from the Salem armory. Not the gun that killed Darby and Gorik, but Gorik's bullet came back as being fired from the same gun that killed Darby. In any case, we've got a warrant on the warehouse. Get your vests on if they aren't already and head over there ASAP. Mia, Leo, and Colton will meet you there."

Emma had already opened the SUV door and dropped inside, Vance rushing to the passenger seat. "Got it. Thanks, Jacinda."

He barely had his seat belt on before she peeled out. "Salem is really haunting you, Last. No pun intended."

"The message is targeted. No confusion there." Her pulse was going faster than the vehicle. Ever since they'd followed that delivery driver to the warehouse, she'd been aching to get inside. And now they finally had their chance.

*Let's finish this.*

Crossing town took only twenty minutes, and when Emma pulled up behind two other Bureau vehicles, she found the rest of their team donning vests on the sidewalk. Well beyond them, the car they'd tailed earlier that day—registered to Little—still sat parked against the curb.

She hurried toward Leo with her own vest half on, half off. "The MPD haven't seen anything, I take it?"

He shook his head, attention moving back to the car they'd followed. "No entrances or exits this way. There's the possibility someone could've left through the back, since all that's fenced off. Back area's connected to multiple warehouses, so it'd just take climbing a fence…but you'd think our delivery guy would've taken his own car with him. He's gotta be in there doing something."

Emma grimaced at the assumption but couldn't disagree. And in a warehouse district like this one, there was no way they could've gotten away with guarding every exit and entrance to warehouses connected to that back area. It would've taken half a precinct to do so.

Colton studied the warehouse, and Emma moved up next to him, giving it another once-over to remind herself of the logistics. He stepped to the left, creating a foot of space between them. She gave him a questioning look—maybe the op had gotten under his skin—but his focus remained on the building.

Corrugated metal siding ran top to bottom along each side, and the only entrance in view was in the front, up a few steps, right alongside a large garage door built for truck entrances. The garage-style door was elevated, a gentle slope allowing entrance.

"Lots of windows peppering the building." Colton shrugged, bouncing on the balls of his feet.

"Yeah." Emma agreed. "But all too high up to be an exit… or to see in."

"No telling if there's a beehive of activity inside, or just a few weapons dealers drowsing over a card game while they guard the goods." Colton looked at her as if asking for an answer to his comment.

She didn't have one.

They moved back toward the group.

"The back's all fenced off?" Vance glanced down at an area map that Mia had just pulled up for viewing. "They checked to make sure there aren't any open gates or cut stretches?"

Mia nodded. "Fence is intact, but there's nothing to keep someone from climbing it and moving between warehouse properties."

Emma adjusted her vest and pulled her gun, holding it to her side. "Okay, here's what's happening. MPD has the perimeter in case anyone flees that way. We'll breach and enter through the one-person door near the corner of the building. I'll take lead."

Colton shook his head. "Aren't we waiting for SWAT?"

Mia pulled up her comms app. "Jacinda says they're tied up on another location. They can send part of a team, but they're still twenty minutes out. We're cleared to do a soft entry if we think it's safe."

Colton's head continued its back-and-forth swivel. "I—"

"Like Mia said, we're cleared for soft entry, so we're not to engage unless forced. If they're inside and dangerous, we pull back and wait for SWAT." Emma stared Colton down.

Colton finally nodded.

Emma glanced at Vance. "You'll take the battering ram and open up our entrance if it's not unlocked. We'll stack like this. I'll enter first, followed by Leo, Mia, and then you, Colton. Vance will take up position in the rear after dropping the battering ram. Everyone got it?"

Neither Colton nor Vance looked thrilled at the idea of entering last, but Vance hefted a battering ram from the back of the SUV and nodded. With everyone else signaling they were ready, the plan was settled.

Emma sprinted from their staging spot to the door near the corner of the warehouse. The team's footsteps thundered behind her, their own sort of guarantee. With this team on her side, the Other could throw anything it wanted to at her, but she had confidence they'd make it out. Not only because they had to, but because they were that good.

*We survived Salem. Just gotta remember that anything after that is a cakewalk, Emma girl.*

At the door, she waited for the others to stack behind her and for Vance to approach with the battering ram in his grip. He signaled he was ready, and she rapped hard on the door with the butt of her gun, knowing her fist would sound like a tired soft-shoe in the space of the large warehouse. "FBI! We're executing a search warrant. If anyone's inside, make yourself known!"

Silence answered, and Emma traded a look with Vance. He seemed ready to batter the door to pieces, already braced and with a grim set to his mouth. Emma held up a hand for him to wait and banged on the door one more time.

"I repeat, this is the FBI! We're coming in with a warrant. Step out now!"

She readied herself for the sound of footsteps or even gunfire, but none answered. When it seemed clear that nobody had heard her—or had no intention of responding—she tried the door handle. It depressed beneath her grip. She gave Vance a quick look, and he tossed the ram to the ground with a clatter and drew his weapon.

She inched the door open, just to prove they wouldn't be barred by a lock or safety chain. Inhaling a deep breath, she made eye contact with each team member stacked behind her, making sure they all registered the open door.

Then she swung it wide and moved into the doorway in one movement, gun up and scanning the room.

The empty space offered up no signs of weapons, let alone weapons *dealers*.

Leo and the others piled up behind her, rushing in to a whole bunch of nothing.

The warehouse was completely empty.

Except for ghosts, that was.

Even as she and her team took in the wide expanse of open cement flooring, the cold of the Other registered on her skin and chilled her hands. On cue, Leo sprinted ahead to the back door of the warehouse, directly across from where she and Colton stood. Doing so, he nearly ran straight through the ghost of Officer Freddy Gorik, whose white-eyed gaze followed him without comment.

And he wasn't alone.

Emma breathed out. "We need to call this in to Jacinda. Colton, you take care of that."

Without waiting for him to reply, she moved on into the open space. Ostensibly to follow Leo, who'd arrived at the back door, flung it open, and stood peering outside. Practically speaking, she wanted to get her ears on what these ghosts were saying.

Around the big, open space, she glimpsed the occasional outline of discolored cement and dust, where large items might once have been stored, but the interior was cleared of whatever it previously held. Scaffolding ran up one wall, leading to a balcony-style office, but it was glass-walled and held nothing but an ancient metal desk. Something to search later, but no one was breathing up there.

So she focused on the dead people.

Besides Officers Gorik and Darby, a dozen other men and women roamed the space. All of them bleeding, having been shot in the chest. A few of them walked together, heads down as they ambled through the area. Others stalked around like annoyed lions in a cage—a habit for Gorik, it seemed—while one young woman sat cross-legged on the cement and wailed about loyalty. "I did everything I was supposed to! I was loyal to her!"

*Her.*

Blood dripped down her forehead as she cried, and Emma glimpsed a gruesome exit wound as she passed by.

Another ghost came within inches of passing through her, dressed in jeans and a white button-down that was mostly dyed red with blood. "I just needed one more chance!" he screamed at thin air as he moved.

Emma turned away to meet Colton's gaze just as he put his phone back in his pocket.

She froze her expression, forcing herself to show no reaction that Colton might interpret as anything out of the ordinary.

She *and* her *is likely my sister.*

Darby's ghost came closer, though he didn't seem to

register her. "The attack's coming. It's coming. Feds by Brooks…"

He moved on, but the chill of his presence remained heavy around Emma, thickening the air and freezing her skin. Behind her, Colton directed MPD to search the upstairs and the perimeter, and ahead of her, Leo came in the back door shaking his head, annoyed.

Emma turned, heading toward the staircase to get closer to Gorik.

He stared at her, hard. "You listening? The Knight's on it. He's everywhere."

Frustration built in Emma's throat. With Colton and MPD present, she couldn't even think of questioning these white-eyed denizens of the Other. Not unless she didn't want her secret really getting out.

*That'd give Colton something to report.*

She bit back a curse and moved on past Gorik toward the door.

If this empty warehouse communicated anything, it was that the Cloaks were well ahead of the FBI and MPD. Ahead of them and preparing for another attack.

Emma gestured for the team to follow her out, speaking low to herself.

*"Feds by Brooks…"* She committed the words to memory. *"The Knight's on it. He's everywhere."* That's what Gorik and Darby had said to her. *"Feds by Brooks…the Knight's… everywhere."* Emma repeated the messages from the slain officers in an effort to decode them.

And that was when it hit her harder than the cold from any of the ghosts. "Leo!"

Leo and Vance came running from where they'd been watching techs gather fingerprints, and Mia and Colton hurried out behind them.

"The Eighth." Emma pulled out her phone in a panic to call Jacinda.

"What about it, Agent Last?" Colton stepped closer.

"Shit. The next attack." Leo read her face. "We gotta go."

Emma called Jacinda.

The SSA answered on the first ring. "Emma—"

"Jacinda, we're still at the warehouse but heading to the Eighth. I have it on," she scanned the faces of the team, Colton's among them, "good authority that they'll be an attack at that location."

"Okay. I hear you. Get everyone and go, now. I'll get ahold of the precinct."

Emma's gut flipped as the ghosts' words echoed in her mind once again.

At the exit, Officer Gorik's ghost gazed and pointed at her angrily, then crossed his arms in a huff.

"What?" She blurted into the air. *Shit.* She turned to find Colton catching up to her. He looked as pale as her otherworldly friends. "You okay?" She hoped he didn't notice her yelling at no one.

"Why wouldn't I be?"

"You look, I dunno, greenish. Like you had bad sushi for lunch."

"I'm fine!" His words came out like angry barks. "But I find it odd we're leaving this crime scene before investigating the second floor. And what 'good authority?' What does that even mean?"

Emma didn't have time for twenty questions. "We can discuss this later. Let's go." That was as good an answer as she could give him. She'd come up with something stronger later.

It hadn't even occurred to her that their unsub would dare attack the station directly—until thirty seconds ago. Hopefully, they wouldn't be too late.

Sliding into the driver's seat, Emma hit the gas even before Vance buckled in. She did a hard U-turn to take the shortest route. Behind her, she glimpsed the other agents doing the same.

Vance read from his phone. "Jacinda says she tried to call the station but no one's answering. 'No one' she texted in all caps. SWAT's on their way."

"I bet they blocked the cell signals to the whole building."

"Why would they do that? Who the hell could've anticipated they'd be so off the rails as to attack an entire police precinct?"

Emma knew the answer to that question, unfortunately. She glanced over at Vance grimly. "Someone who knows I can talk to ghosts."

This told her more than any clue so far that she had a sister, one who would stop at nothing to take her down.

**36**

Chief Brooks Ebenstein doodled nonsensical loops on his legal pad, unable to concentrate after a full day of paperwork, phone calls, and security-footage reviews. In a decade as a police chief at the Eighth, he'd lost only three people in the line of duty—until recently. One of those to a drive-by shooting while the officer was off-duty, one of those to a highway accident during a routine traffic stop, and one of those to a heart attack on the job.

In just days, that figure had nearly tripled.

He pressed the tip of his pen harder into his legal pad, wondering if he could fight past his eyestrain to review the footage sent over by the highway department. It wasn't likely he'd be able to pick out anything suspicious two blocks from the first crime scene, and it was really a job for one of the people on his force, but he needed to be doing something. He couldn't go home to sleep.

And while he was relieved that his conversation last night with Agent Colton Wright had made it clear that the FBI was doing its best to catch this killer, and that the VCU was indeed its most capable team for the job, he didn't feel any better. Not when the asshole wore an FBI windbreaker and cover.

*That has to mean something.*

Hell, just the fact that the agent had requested that meeting proved there were issues within the FBI, if not inside D.C. law enforcement, in general. Whether he'd reassured Brooks that things were in good hands or not, there were too many questions.

And from the last case too.

Starting with Hank Barnaby, someone was doing a damn fine job of trying to pit the PD against the FBI. He truly believed that. Already today, he'd had to remind three of his people that the Feds were on their side, working to catch the killer, just like they were. Short of begging the Bureau for a printout of alibis as delivered by their agents—which Special Agent Emma Last had assured him were being collected—he honestly didn't know what more he could do to convince his officers that any animosity was just playing into the killer's hands.

All this had to be resolved soon. That was all there was to it.

On a normal day, his people wouldn't have doubted the FBI for a second. But right now, everyone was nervous, tense, and ready for the other shoe to drop.

A knock on his door brought his head up. Rookie Officer Gabe Kayne stood there, staring at him nervously. "Sir?"

"Speak up, Officer. What is it?"

He gestured over his shoulder, toward the elevators. "There're some FBI agents downstairs who want to speak with you. Now."

*Finally. Maybe this means they've got something they're pulling me in on.*

Brooks nodded and headed for the elevators without waiting for more. Relief worked its way through his shoulders like a shot of bourbon—just enough to soften the edges. They wouldn't have called him down if they didn't have something. Progress. Answers. Something that might give all this death meaning.

But when the elevator doors slid open on the ground floor, he stopped short.

Six FBI agents stood just beyond the front desk, windbreakers gleaming under the fluorescent lights. All of them in a perfect line, like something out of a movie. But not a face he recognized. Not one.

Brooks squared his shoulders. "Chief Brooks Ebenstein, at your service." He addressed the man in front—a sharp-featured kid, mid-twenties maybe, clean-cut, and slim.

Confident. Too confident. He stood just ahead of the others, clearly in charge.

"I understand you wanted me by name. What can I do for you, Agent…?"

The man smiled.

Didn't answer.

Then, like dominoes falling, every single one of them pulled a weapon.

Brooks had a split second—just enough time to realize none of them had badges in hand—before he threw himself behind the front desk.

Gunshots erupted, deafening and close.

He saw the front desk officer—Sarah, just a year out of academy—slap the panic alarm under the counter, bless her. A half second later, she dropped. A hole in her forehead. Her body hit the floor before he could shout.

Brooks gasped, chest seizing.

A blast of white heat tore through him, somewhere beneath his ribs—so sharp and unexpected, it nearly knocked him unconscious. He fell to one elbow, his other hand clawing for his side, trying to hold something in that wouldn't stay.

Blood poured down his side. Warm, insistent, endless.

More shouts echoed from the hall. The cavalry. Footsteps. His people.

But not all of the footsteps were his people. Others joined the ranks of the faux FBI agents. He couldn't tell how many, but the cacophony that came next told him there was more.

Gunfire opened in return—close, desperate.

Brooks wanted to move. Draw. Fight.

Instead, he slumped back against the wall behind the desk. One leg twisted awkwardly beneath him. Sarah's hand had fallen against his boot, limp and still warm.

He tried to reach for her. Couldn't lift his arm.

The pain grew quieter as the chaos around him grew louder. That terrified him more than anything.

The radio was still on his chest. He pressed it, but no sound came out. Not from him anyway.

He blinked up at the ceiling, bright with flickering lights, and something wet rolled down his cheek. Sweat. Blood. A tear. He couldn't tell anymore.

*I should've seen it coming.*

The thought hit him hard. Not as guilt. Not even as anger. Just a quiet, final disappointment.

Though he fought to inhale, his breath came shallow. Slow. Like a tide pulling away from shore.

Sarah was unmoving beside him. He focused on that. Not the chaos. Not the shooting. Not the dark edges closing in.

Just Sarah.

He'd always told his people to look out for one another.

He stayed with her.

Until he couldn't.

## 37

The fifteen minutes it took to reach the station felt like an eternity.

Sirens sounded from every direction as they got closer. Leo's SUV very nearly kept up with her, and by the time Emma pulled up to a barricade of cop cars a block away, she'd imagined every possible scenario except the one that actually confronted them.

The businesses beyond the barricade were deathly still— all pedestrians must've been hunkering down inside. But beyond that, there was only chaos.

The Eighth Precinct took up a full block and was mostly glass-fronted. Tall concrete pillars supported an overhanging ceiling that held up the second story, and Emma glimpsed a flurry of movement inside. A tight barricade curved in a semicircle across the door. In front of the precinct, cop cars were parked in a long line, angling into the intersection, creating a wider second barricade. Cops crouched behind their cruisers, some of them standing to fire on the precinct as Emma and the team arrived.

Out of the SUV, she and Vance headed down the

sidewalk toward the inner barricade, keeping close to the office building on their right, the same side as the precinct. The rest of the team snaked along behind them. She glimpsed an FBI agent—or, rather, what looked like an FBI agent—ducking back behind one of the pillars fronting the station after firing out at the street. The weirdness of it caught her breath, but there wasn't time to slow down and reflect.

"Don't forget, we look like public enemy number one to many of these officers," she shouted over her shoulder.

These people in FBI gear firing on cops were the miscreants in this scenario, no question. And whether the cops outside belonged to this precinct or not, Emma had no clue, but that seemed truly irrelevant at the moment. The cops were on their side, and the false flag agents were not.

Cops were mostly sheltering in place, with not enough of a pause between gunfire to allow real retaliation. But they appeared to all be alive and unharmed.

Hurrying down the sidewalk with the rest of the team behind her, Vance directly at her back, Emma kept to the side of the buildings as best she could. The precinct was a five-story building, but she only spotted movement inside the first-floor lobby. Street-level, where the doors were shattered.

Ahead of her, she spotted another false flag FBI agent duck out from a first-floor window and aim his gun in their direction.

Her breath locked in her chest. The man wore an FBI windbreaker. *Her* windbreaker. For half a second, her brain refused to make the call.

But his gun was up—and aimed.

She fired.

The crack split the air, and the agent—no, the imposter—crumpled in the doorway, one arm inside the station, the rest sprawled on the steps like he couldn't decide which side he belonged on.

Emma didn't look away until she was sure he was dead. She couldn't afford to—not yet.

Vance cursed behind her. "So there's more than one impersonator. Little could've killed Gorik, while another one of these scumbags took down Darby." He breathed fast as they moved, with his attention on the street in case someone swept around the corner.

Emma gave him a quick glance, nodding. "You recognize anyone?"

"Yep. Gidney!" Vance waved over an officer who'd been hunkered down behind a nearby cruiser, waiting for a chance to fire.

She darted a glance behind her before sprinting toward the team.

Leo gripped her arm to steady her as she skidded to a stop, gasping. "Officer Gidney, talk to us."

"They've been firing nonstop for the last five minutes. They've…"

"Catch your breath." Emma met her gaze, forcing herself to take even breaths, setting an example. She put one hand to her chest, apparently willing her breath in a more controlled fashion. It seemed to have worked. Emma smiled, channeling a calm she didn't feel. "Okay, Officer Gidney. I'm Special Agent Emma Last. Now, how can we get in without going through the front?"

The cop pointed down the alley just ahead of them. It ran alongside the precinct, but a tall fence blocked the way partially down. "There's a security gate. I can get you in with a code and my badge."

Leo clapped her on the shoulder. "Good. You stay in the middle of our team as we move, you hear me?"

Gidney nodded.

While Emma and Leo covered the street, Gidney, along with Vance, Mia, and Colton, sprinted across the street and stacked against the corner. Another false flag agent could be seen just within the building, but his focus was on the cops in the street. When he aimed on a cruiser, Leo shot him down, yelling out in rage as he sprinted for cover.

He sounded more like a bear than her partner, but the anger in his voice steadied Emma.

They had the enemy in their sights now, and it was time to take their city back and protect their fellow members of law enforcement before this went any further. Shooting, as soon as they'd determined whose side someone was on, was a given. This was a free-for-all by all appearances, and the horror on everyone's faces was proof of it.

Emma sprinted for the rest of the team. When she landed with her back on the wall, she turned to Colton. "You okay?" He still looked like he'd eaten some bad fish when he'd been so cool and collected at the op. It wasn't adding up.

He nodded, swallowing hard. "I'm good. You? Though a bit strange firing at…FBI."

"Don't think of it like that." Emma spoke fast, her focus on the street.

"Could you tell if either of those men we just shot down was Norman Little?" Mia yelled over a new volley of gunfire erupting, but Emma understood her well enough.

She shook her head. "Neither. Leo's guy was beefy, squat, and white. The guy I shot was Hispanic. And Little is thin, tall, and white. Mid-twenties, blond."

Emma nodded toward the gate blocking the alley halfway down. "Let's go. We can talk while we move."

Just within her sight, a cop stationed behind one of the cars popped up, firing on a target within the precinct. His hat was knocked off on his way back down. He disappeared behind the car. Another D.C. officer fallen. Emma hoped against all odds it wasn't a bullet that dropped him.

She swallowed her horror. "We have no way of knowing how many false flag agents are inside. We have to be alert to anyone pretending and be ready for anything…"

"And we don't know if we've got any real Feds in there." Mia grimaced. "And we have to assume there are cops fighting them from inside as well as out front."

At the gate, Gidney pulled out her badge and scanned it. As the gate slid open, she pointed farther down the building. "That'll put us by the holding cells, behind the lobby."

Emma nodded the go-ahead.

They rushed through as soon as the gap was wide enough. Then they used Officer Gidney's key card to unlock the back entrance.

Leo gripped the handle and opened the door just enough to keep the lock from reengaging. "Officer Gidney, what are we walking into exactly?"

She spoke in a rush. "There's a small entry area. It won't fit all of us. Then another door we can open with my ID. Then a hall that runs along the holding cells. It snakes back on itself, doing a U-turn. That'll put us here." She pointed to the wall maybe five feet from where they stood, facing the lobby.

"And after that?"

"Then there'll be a hall running forward. An opening on the left, fronting the lobby, and the glass-walled hallway on the right, opening to the bullpen, coming up opposite, or before, the lobby. There are doors at each turn, interior offices and whatnot."

Emma pictured it as the woman spoke. Maybe she hadn't had reason to be in the holding cells before now, but they had no reason to expect false flag agents waiting for them there.

Leo took the woman's ID, nodding at Emma, and the two of them made ready to move forward together.

Emma adjusted her grip on her gun, then she and Leo led the way. She scanned the holding cells as they moved through the short maze of halls and offices, all empty, as shouts and screams and gunshots echoed from farther inside.

At the corner, which would lead them around to the lobby, Emma looked at their small group. Vance breathed heavily, and Mia was wide-eyed and thin-lipped, but everyone gestured their readiness.

Emma swallowed. "Make sure you're positive of hostile intent before you fire, but nobody trust the uniforms you see. Understood?"

Everyone nodded.

Emma turned back to Leo, and he put the ID against the scanner until it flashed green and pulled the door slightly open. Then he slipped his foot into the crack in the door. Mia grabbed it, ready to fling it open on cue. He counted down with his free hand.

*Three. Two. One.*

Leo erupted through the door, with Emma on his heels.

Most of the glass in the hall lay shattered on the tile. A cop at the front desk had slumped out of her chair, another one collapsed on the floor by her side.

Dangerous anger eclipsed her as a handful of false flag agents turned their guns on them. One she recognized as Norman Little.

Two of them fired right at them—neither one Little—and she shot back.

Her man fell, and the other next to him dropped a second later, Leo's bullet having hit him in the throat. As Emma confirmed the kills, she watched Little aim beyond them. He'd had a clear shot at either her or Leo, but he seemed to be searching for a target, unlike his buddies firing wildly.

Mia let out a stark cry of warning behind her.

A shot rang out as fire jumped from the muzzle of Little's weapon.

Colton screamed. "What the fuck, Little!"

His words were nearly lost as Vance yelled for them to run.

Emma twisted and followed her team. She slammed into the wall at the end of the hall and was yanked sideways by an arm. It was Leo pulling her to safety.

Vance and Mia had dragged Colton over, her hands pressed to his thigh, screaming his name while arterial blood sprayed upward. Vance removed his belt and created a fast tourniquet, as Mia glanced up at Emma, face wet with tears and some of Colton's blood splatter. "He insisted on coming in last behind me and Vance. I didn't even see it coming."

Vance cursed again.

Leo was breathing heavily with adrenaline and firing around the corner. "These bastards are going to pay for this."

Other cops were firing on Little from the stairwell.

Officer Gidney knelt beside Mia, checking Colton's pulse, as Leo and Vance took turns shooting around the corner, attempting to take down the remaining false flag agents. If Emma didn't miss her guess, there were three others aside from Little.

Emma leaned past Leo to take a shot—and there was Little, making a break for it. He slammed into a side door, knocking his gun free before barreling through it to the outside.

*What the hell?*

Emma glanced at her team. She was needed here, but they had to get Little, or this might just be the precursor to another massacre.

Mia waved her forward. "Go! Take point. I'm behind you!"

"Cover me!" she yelled, only waiting long enough for a volley of bullets to drive the false agents down. She took off, shoving by the desks, and hit the exit door at a full sprint.

She expected Mia to be right behind her. But by the time she hit the door, Mia was under fire again. She met her friend's eye.

"Go!" Mia shouted.

Little had the answers.

And that meant nothing could stand in the way of her bringing him down.

**38**

---

The door opened onto an alley running behind the station, and Emma glimpsed Norman Little's figure as he swerved around a corner and away from the chaos.

She sprinted forward, gun at low ready as she screamed into her mic. "In pursuit of Little! Heading northbound away from precinct toward Fifth!"

The next street had been cleared of everything but a few dumpsters, but Little had used those to his advantage—she couldn't see him anywhere. His footsteps sounded in the distance.

As she rounded a corner, she spotted him, a block away and zigzagging. They were far enough away from the station that pedestrian traffic was now a concern, and it was impossible to fire on him. Plus, there was a chance he wasn't armed at all. He'd dropped his gun, so unless he had a backup, she had that as an advantage.

Emma put on an extra burst of speed, nearly knocking over two teenagers trying to film the chase instead of getting out of the way.

When she catapulted around a building in his direction,

she caught Little screaming into the phone as he twisted into a run. "I took him down! Now help me!" Without looking, he jetted out into the street from the sidewalk and bounced off the front of a slow-moving car.

Emma screamed, "FBI!" at the terrified driver before dodging around the vehicle.

Little was still hustling but with a clear limp. He ran left between two buildings.

She triggered her mic. "Suspect turned west onto an alley between JoJo's Flower Shop and a residential street!"

As she turned the corner, an arm caught her in the chest, clotheslining her and knocking her off her feet. She flung her arms out to either side to break the fall. Still, she hit the asphalt hard, and her gun went flying as Little leaped on top of her, wielding a knife.

"You must be Emma." He grinned, breathing hard and holding the knife above her chest, ready to strike.

With a jerk of her hips, Emma knocked him sideways and twisted from under his attack. She rolled just before the knife struck the ground.

Little tried to correct his aim, but the limp was slowing him down. His leg appeared to be pretty injured, possibly fractured from the impact with the car.

Emma landed a punch directly to his leg, and Little howled, dropping his knife. As he reached for it, she delivered a hard blow to his ribs.

He curled into a fetal position as she continued to strike him, letting out one animalistic scream after another before finally pleading with her to stop. "I give up! I surrender. Please!"

Emma caught her breath and rolled Little onto his stomach. Knee in his back, she grappled with his hands and clicked her cuffs shut.

"You're under arrest, Norman Little. Now get to your feet, you piece of shit."

# 39

Emma pictured the dead rookie cop who'd begun this case, Officer Greg Darby, and remembered the praise Chief Ebenstein had given him. She pictured Officer Freddy Gorik. Finally, she pictured the chief, in the ICU now in critical condition. Her whole team had gotten to know him over the last few weeks. The man was devoted to his job, to his officers, and to his faith in her people to find the man who now sat behind this door.

She was almost certain he hadn't fired the bullet that killed Darby, but it was going to take a lot to convince her he didn't kill Gorik. They needed the other shooter. And she intended to interrogate him until she left with a name.

Thanks to Brooks Ebenstein, all his officers were vested up, as they should've been, including the chief himself. The death count was one so far, with one officer in critical condition and three more stable, recovering at home. Ebenstein was hit, however, at point-blank range. The bullet had gone in right under his left arm, above the vest. But Emma was still hopeful.

And there was Colton Wright, their newest team

member. He'd lost a lot of blood, but it appeared he was going to be okay. Mia had headed over to check on him while Vance finished looking into Agent Gavin Knight from Boston and retired Agent Ron Knight out of Connecticut. There was another shooter out there, and that name was their only lead—until she got Norman Little to talk, that was.

After taking in a slow breath and exhaling, Emma entered the interrogation room.

Norman Little didn't look like anything special. Just over six feet. Blond and slim, with handsome enough features and the run-of-the-mill cockiness of so many other twenty-four-year-old men. Only the annoyed set to his lips, the bandages around his ribs, and the brace around his leg gave him away as something different. They'd also bandaged his hands when he complained of road rash from their fight in the alley. She'd had paper cuts that had looked worse, but whatever.

Paramedics had bandaged him up and handed him directly back into Bureau custody, not wanting to give him any more courtesy than necessary.

For the audio and visual recording, Emma stated the date, time, and those present. She then pulled out the seat across from Little and dropped into it in one practiced motion, staring the man down. The barest flinch around his eyes told her he recognized her as the one who cuffed him. Hell, he'd said her name during the takedown.

"How are your ribs? And your leg?"

His eyes widened a touch. "They fucking hurt."

Emma let him wonder for a moment before giving him a big smile. "That's good to hear. Now, on to business. Who paid you? We found sizable bank deposits and a large amount of cash in a subway locker opened with that key you had in your pocket."

He swallowed. "I'm not saying anything to you."

"We found calls from an unlisted number on your phone

also, and we know you're connected to the weapons manufacturer." She paused, holding in her annoyance. "If you give up some names, maybe we can be a little lenient on you. Avoid the death penalty, at least."

He smirked. "Now you're lying. You have no control over that. If you're trying to bargain and threaten, you've already lost. The death penalty's for killers anyway."

*This asshole tried to kill Colton, and now he's got the gall to taunt us.*

She couldn't swear to it, but Emma didn't think she'd ever in her life wished so badly that she could use physical violence against a man she'd arrested. Not like this. With so many good people's funerals on the horizon, and the potential for so much more damage to come, her veins felt pressurized by the very knowledge that this man could give her every answer she needed.

They'd lost some heroes who'd lived and breathed to make this city a better place. And this bastard had laid his hands directly to that effort. She needed, with every bit of her soul, to make sure nothing like the recent destruction happened again.

But to do that, she needed him to give up his secrets. The secrets of the Cloaks, of the other shooter, and of his benefactor.

And right now, it appeared he wasn't going to give up anything.

"Let's try something else." She sat back, mirroring his posture. "How did you know my name, Norman Little?"

He smiled, wide enough to show a long-chipped tooth that Emma dearly wished she could knock right out. The man wasn't just confident but also amused.

"Loyalty will get you nowhere."

"You don't know the meaning of loyalty." He smacked his lips, showing that chipped tooth again.

Emma lifted a shoulder. "Why do you say that?"

"The Bureau employed you. Has it tested you? Made you prove your fealty to a cause higher than yourself? Forced you to shed your blood and prove yourself a loyal exterminator over and over again?"

"Loyalty means a lot to you, hmm?" She stared at him, waiting. "Did you have to prove yourself to someone?"

He pressed his lips closed.

She gripped the apatite Marigold had given her, biding her time and counting to herself like Oren would've told her to do.

When her blood pressure eased, she mirrored his smile. "Let's go back to the guns, Norman, and the bullets that killed two cops, one that was your brother-in-law. We both know where you got them."

She watched as his neck grew flush. He remained mute.

"You think we don't know that Greg Darby's wife, Jeannie, is your half-sister on your mom's side? That your father, Barry, a member of the Cloaks, is in prison? That your RAV4 was seen leaving the scene of Gorik's death? That's the death penalty right there."

"I didn't kill Gorik!"

"And if that can't stick, we'll take you down for Darby if you don't talk." Emma leaned in, voice low. "Between you and me, I know you didn't kill him. But it'll be easy to convince a jury otherwise."

What she desperately wanted, though, more than anything, was to hear him say the name of his benefactor.

Little only observed her, bandaged hands relaxed in their cuffs on the table.

Emma tried to forget the question bothering her most. "I'm waiting, Norman." She allowed just a hint of impatience to enter her tone. "But I won't wait forever, and that means your chance for some leniency is winding down. You'd be surprised how much credence federal prosecutors give to arresting agents' recommendations. And, right now, you're the only arrestee in a case that's seen multiple MPD officers gunned down in the line of duty and killed. There's no question that the U.S. attorney will push for the death penalty."

"Lot of big words for a Bureau grunt." He shrugged. "And besides, you of all people should know some of these answers."

Emma searched his features, but nothing about him seemed familiar. She could swear she hadn't met the man before, and she certainly didn't recognize him from Salem. But if that was the case…

"What do you mean by that, Norman? Me 'of all people?'"

"You look just like her." That grin showed again, even wider.

*My mystery sibling.*

*She* is *the one behind this. Dammit!*

Emma's pulse throbbed, and she clamped her fist tight around the crystal in her grip, hoping it might center her like Marigold had suggested.

"I look like 'her?'" She stared at him, waiting. "Tell me about 'her,' Norman. She seems important to you."

He shifted in his seat, head cocked. Appearing curious for the first time.

"How did you meet your boss? She's your boss, right? This mysterious 'her' you mentioned."

"She found me." The chipped tooth reappeared. "Through a mutual friend."

*A mutual friend?*

Celeste Foss wouldn't be called her "friend." And nothing in Little's history suggested he'd had any interaction with that evil woman prior to her death.

"She gave me a chance when nobody else would."

Norman rubbed one of his bandaged hands on the table, grimacing as he did.

Emma was glad the wound itched, and her lip curled up ever so slightly.

"She's more powerful than you can imagine, I promise. And I'll remain loyal to her, because she never gave up on me."

Emma shook her head, smiling even as her blood went a touch colder. Maybe going back to his refrain of blasted loyalty would help, since he kept harping on it. "Loyalty is important to you, clearly. Tell me about that."

He squinted at her. "You wouldn't understand."

"I wouldn't?" She shrugged, mirroring his slouch. "I'd understand wanting to prove yourself to someone you respect. Anyone worth anything has been there. Has had to prove themselves. You mentioned that earlier."

He nodded, a move just barely perceptible. "I didn't think you were listening."

Emma held her smile, though she wanted to scream.

With a twitch of his lip, he leaned forward.

She did the same.

"I've been proving myself loyal all my life. To my dad, though he never paid attention."

"Your dad and the Cloaks, I imagine." Emma kept a straight face as his eyes widened. "Is that what you mean?"

"Those assholes, the Cloaks…they never gave me a chance any more than my dad did. No matter what I did. And then she came along and earned my trust, and then I proved myself to her, big-time. We're loyal to each other now, no matter what you do with me. No way will I answer to you over her."

"She has no sway in court or in prison, Norman. You should rethink that."

The chip in his tooth showed again through a grin that

had only gotten wider. "I have a feeling she'll end up on top, so I'll take my chances."

Emma waited a moment, searching for something more she might say to make the man talk, but the way he watched her said it all. This asshole was ready to go to prison for the woman who'd given him his marching orders.

And Emma was done fighting with him. She had another shooter to find. Maybe the way to that killer was through the "mutual friend" of which he spoke.

She nodded at his right hand. "That your writing hand?"

He narrowed his eyes. "You want me to write you a blood oath? Promise my loyalty to her so you can pass it on?"

Emma steeled her expression. The blood oath between her mother, Celeste, and Monique was the impetus for so much strife. "Not likely."

Trying to forget his phrasing, she pressed a pen and legal pad toward him. "I need a written statement. Say whatever cryptic bullshit you want, and then you can go rot in a jail cell for all I care. Until the U.S. attorney's office brings the charges that will most likely see you on a table receiving a lethal injection. I doubt your boss will raise a finger to help you. I doubt she'll even blink."

He observed her for a moment before nodding. "I proved myself to her, so I don't mind telling you about it."

The man awkwardly picked up the pen, cuff rattling, and began a loose, scrawling sentence. He wrote and wrote and wrote. Emma picked out the word "loyalty" more than once, along with "allegiance" and "proved myself." And, of course, there was that word, "exterminator." She wondered if he even mentioned lives he'd stolen, but she let him write in silence.

When he filled the page, he dropped the pen.

Emma pulled the notepad to her. His handwriting was stupidly neat, and that somehow annoyed her, but it also allowed her to quickly determine that he'd written out exactly what he'd told her, and something of a mini-essay on the meaning of loyalty. But of her sister or the other shooter, he hadn't written a word.

Still. The wording was…interesting.

She pocketed the thought, keeping her gaze neutral, then left the room.

Outside, she leaned against the wall beside the door and reexamined the writing.

Leo exited the observation room door. "Anything there you didn't already hear?"

"No, but look at this." She angled the legal pad so he'd be able to follow along as she read aloud. "'My boss recruited me and gave me a chance. I proved myself by exterminating the dregs of society and even one of our own, and now I will be loyal.'"

He frowned. "Sounds robotic."

"That's what I was thinking. Like maybe he's parroting someone?"

"You mean the 'she' who looks 'just like you?'"

That was exactly who Emma was thinking of. "Yeah. But I'm bothered by something."

"Talk to me." He leaned against the wall, curiosity and concern blanketing his features in equal measure.

"This mutual friend Little spoke of…"

"Which couldn't be Celeste Foss. People don't call their mothers their friends." Leo cocked his head. "Do you think he met a mutual friend of yours and *his*?"

Emma hadn't thought of that.

*A mutual friend…of ours.*

"I have no connection to this lowlife, none whatsoever. Except in the undercover op, when I went as Shelly Kern. Would Darko be our mutual connection?"

Colton, posing as Rick Dwyer, was her only real connection to the Cloaks.

Jack Darko…

Emma reviewed that interaction, especially when Darko had said to Colton, "*Damn, you've got a type.*"

"Damn, you've got a type." Emma mumbled it out loud.

Leo's eyebrow shot up. "What's that?"

Emma shook her head. It wasn't adding up. "When we were at Darko's, the guy looked me up and down and then told Colton he had a type. Like I looked just like someone he dated."

"What are you saying?"

"Did you notice him turn green at the warehouse when I knew they were attacking the Eighth?"

"He might've been confused. Obviously, a ghost told you, right? So he was probably wondering how the hell you could possibly know that…or why we'd all just go along with it." Leo shrugged in a way that said he'd have thought Emma sounded nuts, too, had he not known Emma communed with the dead.

Emma ran a hand through her hair. "Little had a chance to shoot us at the precinct, and he didn't."

"He aimed past us and took down Colton. I logged that too."

And that was when it hit her like a bullet to the chest. "Leo! Oh my god, you were right! He's the 'friend' Norman Little and I have in common."

Just as she spoke those words, Vance came barreling their way. "We've got our killer. We gotta get to Our Savior's, now! It's—"

Emma finished his thought.

"Colton."

## 40

Emma was behind the wheel of the FBI-issue SUV in what felt like two seconds flat. Leo rode shotgun, and Vance hopped in the back seat. She was out of the garage before either one of them belted in.

Leo took his phone out, and their SSA picked up on the first ring. "Jacinda, it's Emma, Vance, and me. We're on our way to Our Savior's. We have it on good authority that Colton Wright is our killer—"

"Jacinda, it's Vance." Emma could see in the rearview that the man was practically coming apart at the seams. "The retired agent, Ron Knight, was responsible for taking down Crooked Carl Kinkade."

"The serial killer from the early 2000s. Yeah, rings a bell. He was one of our most wanted."

"And Knight ended up getting the Meritorious Service Medal when he retired."

"Bring this around to Colton. And, Emma, slow down!" Jacinda barked.

Leo gave the phone a look that indicated the SSA had given an impossible order.

"Yeah, Vance, connect the dots. I want to hear this." Emma chimed in as the speedometer ticked past eighty-five.

"It was a car chase that wasn't without casualties that took the serial killer down. Though stopping Crooked Kinkade likely saved dozens of women's lives, a civilian was killed. A Camille Wright."

Emma gasped. "Colton's mother?"

Vance nodded. "The kid was eight years old. Family got a hefty settlement—"

"But no amount of money in the world can bring back a child's mother." Leo slumped in his seat.

Emma saw him deflate in the corner of her eye. Leo was around that age when he lost both parents. "Colton's been planning this his whole life." She veered right, getting off the exit to the hospital.

"With a degree from Yale in International Securities Studies to support this theory. He's our guy, Jacinda, and—"

"Okay, Vance, you need to calm down too. This is all still circumstantial, and he was in pretty bad shape when he went in earlier, so go in easy."

"Jacinda!" Vance spoke harshly. "Mia's there with him right now." He tapped the screen of his own phone. "And she's not picking up!"

Emma turned the wheel hard. "Jacinda, we're pulling in now. Keep you posted."

Leo hung up. "Dammit." He huffed. "I knew it, I fucking knew it. I sensed it."

"You're not alone, Leo, but we can't think about that now." Vance was suddenly the voice of reason. "We've got to get to Mia." He tried her again. "C'mon, babe, pick up the phone!" And he was his hotheaded self again.

They'd made it inside the south wing of the hospital.

Vance flashed his badge at the nurses' station.

A sweet-faced woman with her hair in a tight bun looked

up at him. "Are you here to visit Agent Wright? He has a visitor currently, and we generally don't like there to be more than one."

Emma watched as Vance got redder under the collar, the skin inching toward purple. He looked like he might leap over the counter. Leo set a hand on his arm.

"This is FBI business." Emma gave her a *this is important* look. "We won't be in there long. His room number?"

"It's 306. Down this hall, then go left down the second hall, then left again. It's the third door down on the right."

Vance stalked off. "Could it be any farther away?"

Emma and Leo speed-walked behind him.

Without another word between them, they veered left, then left…barreling down the hallways until what sounded like a scuffle made them skid to a stop. Had a lunch tray hit the floor?

"Did you hear—?"

A woman screamed, "Get off me!"

Vance busted into room 306 an instant later, with Leo behind him and Emma coming up the rear, gun drawn.

"Mia!" The terror in Vance's shout clutched at Emma's heart.

Mia was under Colton. He had her straddled and was strangling her with the cord from one of the monitors. She had her hand on her weapon, except his knee was holding her arm down. And her free arm wasn't doing much more than causing a few surface scratches, certainly nothing to deter him from cutting off her oxygen.

Vance pushed the man off her with a boot to the chest and slid Mia into his arms, holding her and untangling the cord.

Mia was red-faced, choking, with tears pouring down her cheeks, but she seemed to be okay.

Colton stood, spinning awkwardly with his bad leg—

looking for a weapon, it seemed—and then he tried to make some kind of a run for it. Leo got him with a surprise left hook. Blood from his nose exploded all over them both.

Emma trained her gun on him. "Colton Wright, you're under arrest for the murders of Officers Greg Darby and Freddy Gorik."

Colton's eyes were wild. He was still thinking of fleeing. There was only one way out. Plowing through her. And there was no chance of that happening.

He stood there for an instant, catching his breath as Mia coughed a few more times, catching hers. Without a word, he wiped the blood from his nose and smeared it down his patient gown.

For the first time, Emma noticed he was half dressed. The rest of his belongings were in a bag on the bed. She put it all together. It looked like he was about to flee when Mia must've walked in on him.

Colton stepped toward her with a limp. Blood seeped into the bandage covering his inner thigh, looking like a rusty Rorschach blot. The man was falling apart but seemed unfazed. Leo lifted his fists, ready to knock him right out if need be.

The agent stayed where he was and looked Emma in the eyes. "You'll never catch her, Agent Last. She's smarter than all of you."

She pulled out her cuffs. "I bet you felt that way, too, Agent Wright. Up until two minutes ago. Now get back in bed."

He pivoted with a limp and a groan.

Emma holstered her weapon, walked over, and cuffed him to the bed rail. "The next place you're off to is a comfy prison infirmary."

They had their guy.

And Emma couldn't wait to interrogate him.

## 41

Emma gripped the wheel of her car tighter as she spoke. "Bluetooth, call Marigold."

*"Calling Marigold."* The mechanical voice disappeared with a few beeps, then the sound of a ringtone came through. Followed, for the second time since Emma had left the Bureau, by Marigold's voicemail.

"Bluetooth, hang up."

The sound of silence engulfed the car just as Emma pulled into a parking spot in her complex and sighed. Certainly, filling up Marigold's answering service with "call me" messages was pointless, but Emma had really hoped to see her today.

"It's a Saturday." She muttered to herself, gathering her things from the passenger seat and stepping out into the light rain just starting to fall. "She's probably in back-to-back readings for nervous housewives and lovelorn college students."

That notion didn't quite feel true, though. When had Marigold *not* answered Emma's calls?

Granted, Emma usually called at night, at odd hours…but Marigold had made it clear that Emma's situation was a top priority and that she considered her a friend. The little crystal in her pocket felt like some proof of that even as Emma gripped it in thought.

It was the weekend. Not everyone worked twenty-four seven like she and her team seemed to. She hadn't gotten to sink her teeth into Colton Wright as she'd hoped. His blood pressure dropped off a cliff within minutes of her cuffing him.

Hospital staff had needed to sedate him. The bullet wound had reopened in the scuffle, and he'd needed seventeen stitches to close the thick layer of skin his accomplice, Norman Little, had blown through. Two officers would be outside his door in rotation during his recovery.

As she stepped out of the car, Emma forced herself to shove away her worry about Marigold and think about the case, at least briefly. Going through Norman Little's apartment and determining what trace evidence there might've been took a couple days. Colton's home was still being processed. Because he was a federal agent, the teams were being more careful with potentially sensitive information.

Chances of finding evidence of her alleged sister at Colton's seemed high.

If they were lucky.

And then there was the aftermath. Jacinda had talked earlier about how the mayor was already planning for a major ceremony to honor the fallen MPD officers. Emma and the whole team would be present, front and center, along with the cops who'd aided their team.

Maybe worrying about Marigold was the least stressful of her options at this moment.

*Just let your brain rest, Emma girl. For one day.*

That wouldn't happen, of course. Even if she wanted it to.

So tonight, she'd focus on the Other and getting to the bottom of this disaster to find her sister. And then she'd focus on honoring the dead and call Jacinda to find out if there was any way she could help.

She took the stairs fast, already deciding to go back on what she'd just told herself. She'd change clothes and then call Marigold again. And if she didn't answer...maybe she'd pick up those fancy herbal lattes Marigold told her about and simply show up on her doorstep.

But Emma smelled it as soon as she opened the stairwell door and moved into the hallway. *Blood.* The distinct, coppery scent of it.

She swallowed, hand near her gun now, as she scanned the area. No sign of anything having been disturbed. Up and down the hall, the carpeted floor was clear of any signs of blood too.

Except outside her door.

*Dammit!*

Her jaw dropped as she approached, a sudden whimper clogging her throat. She knelt in front of her apartment door and stared at the grotesque display welcoming her home.

A hand. A woman's right hand. The fingers still curled slightly, as if trying to cling to life. On the middle finger, a beautiful sterling-silver ring, an apatite in the center.

Apatite. For clarity. Truth. Equilibrium.

The hand belonged to Emma's last shield between this world and the Other.

The hand belonged to Marigold.

*The End*
*To be continued...*

Thank you for reading.
All of Emma Last series books can be found on Amazon.

# ACKNOWLEDGMENTS

The past few years have been a whirlwind of change, both personally and professionally, and I find myself at a loss for the right words to express my profound gratitude to those who have supported me on this remarkable journey. Yet, I am compelled to try.

To my sons, whose unwavering support has been my bedrock, granting me the time and energy to transform my darkest thoughts into words on paper. Your steadfast belief in me has never faltered, and watching each of you grow, welcoming the wonderful daughters you've brought into our family, has been a source of immense pride and joy.

Embarking on the dual role of both author and publisher has been an exhilarating, albeit challenging, adventure. Transitioning from the solitude of writing to the dynamic world of publishing has opened new horizons for me, and I'm deeply grateful for the opportunity to share my work directly with you, the readers.

I extend my heartfelt thanks to the entire team at Mary Stone Publishing, the same dedicated group who first recognized my potential as an indie author years ago. Your collective efforts, from the editors whose skillful hands have polished my words to the designers, marketers, and support staff who breathe life into these books, have been instrumental in resonating deeply with our readers. Each of you plays a crucial role in this journey, not only nurturing my growth but also ensuring that every story reaches its full potential. Your dedication, creativity, and finesse have been nothing short of invaluable.

However, my deepest gratitude is reserved for you, my beloved readers. You ventured off the beaten path of traditional publishing to embrace my work, investing your most precious asset—your time. It is my sincerest hope that this book has enriched that time, leaving you with memories that linger long after the last page is turned.

With all my love and heartfelt appreciation,

*Mary*

# ABOUT THE AUTHOR

Nestled in the serene Blue Ridge Mountains of East Tennessee, Mary Stone crafts her stories surrounded by the natural beauty that inspires her. What was once a home filled with the lively energy of her sons has now become a peaceful writer's retreat, shared with cherished pets and the vivid characters of her imagination.

As her sons grew and welcomed wonderful daughters-in-law into the family, Mary's life entered a quieter phase, rich with opportunities for deep creative focus. In this tranquil environment, she weaves tales of courage, resilience, and intrigue, each story a testament to her evolving journey as a writer.

From childhood fears of shadowy figures under the bed to a profound understanding of humanity's real-life villains, Mary's style has been shaped by the realization that the most complex antagonists often hide in plain sight. Her writing is characterized by strong, multifaceted heroines who defy traditional roles, standing as equals among their peers in a world of suspense and danger.

Mary's career has blossomed from being a solitary author to establishing her own publishing house—a significant milestone that marks her growth in the literary world. This expansion is not just a personal achievement but a reflection of her commitment to bring thrilling and thought-provoking stories to a wider audience. As an author and publisher, Mary continues to challenge the conventions of the thriller genre, inviting readers into gripping tales filled with serial killers, astute FBI agents, and intrepid heroines who confront peril with unflinching bravery.

Each new story from Mary's pen—or her publishing house—is a pledge to captivate, thrill, and inspire, continuing the legacy of the imaginative little girl who once found wonder and mystery in the shadows.

Discover more about Mary Stone on her website.
www.authormarystone.com

Printed in Great Britain
by Amazon